Real Love from a Boss

The Tale of Kon & Sapphire 2

Nechol

Christina "Chrissy" Wallace

My heart thumped rapidly in my chest and my palms were clammy as fuck as I tried my best to grip the steering wheel and whip in and out of traffic. I couldn't believe the shit I'd just done, but that bitch Sapphire had the shit coming. Kon had me fucked up when he called and told me that Sapphire was pregnant with his child and threatened me to stay the fuck away from her. I knew that if she was to bring that baby into the world, there was going to be no fucking way I was going to be able to get her the fuck away from my man.

When Kon found out what I'd done, I knew it was going to be the end of shit for me, that's why I prayed that hoe died right there in that fucking parking lot before anyone was able to find her.

My mind was all over the fucking place and I didn't want to take my ass home in case Kon caught wind of what I'd done, so I pulled over to the side of the road and called Thugga. He was the only person that I knew was going to be able to help me. If I called and told Serenity what the fuck I did, she was going to have everything in the world to say.

That motherfucker was supposed to be on my fucking side, but sometimes with the way she acted, you'd think that she wasn't. I loved my best friend to death, but sometimes, I wanted to hang her ass up by her fucking head.

"Hello?" Thugga answered. I hadn't spoken to him since I told him that I was going to help him get Kon back.

"Hey, it's Chrissy." I palmed my forehead, realizing that he probably already knew who I was before he answered the phone. It wasn't the first time I've called his phone.

"I already knew that from the caller ID."

"Sorry." I glanced in my rearview mirror to make sure no one was following me. I was paranoid as hell after stabbing Sapphire. Lucky for me, no one was in the parking lot to see me, or else I would have been getting hauled off to prison right about now.

"Is everything okay?"

"Not really. I did something..."

"What?"

"I can't say over the phone. Can I come over?" I didn't know this man from a can of paint, yet I was about to go running to him for help.

"Okay. I'll text you the address."

The phone hung up and I sat there, heart racing in my chest, waiting for his message, so I could get the hell out of there. The moment the phone beeped, and I placed his address in the GPS, I sped off.

It didn't take me long to make it to Thugga's location. When I arrived, he was standing on the porch with a cigar dangling from his lips. He was dressed down in a pair of black joggers and a white t-shirt, looking hella' different from the last time I encountered him.

I sat there, watching him for a moment, trying my best to regulate my breathing. "What the fuck are you so nervous about?" I asked myself. I had done something that I had been wanting to do for the fucking longest, but it felt so... wrong in a sense. All I could think about was Kon taking my baby away from me or being locked up for life if he found out. I needed a fucking alibi or something.

Tap!

I jumped and my heart got caught in my throat. Thugga stood at my window with a mug on his handsome face. He scared the shit out of me. My hand pressed against my chest as I gazed at him.

"What the fuck are you doing? are you going to get out of the car?"

Letting the window down, I said, "You scared the shit outta me."

"You're the one that pulled in the driveway and didn't get out of the car. Are you going to tell me what the hell is going on?"

Feeling my heart skip beats, I let the window back up, and get out of the car. I gazed up into his eyes and debated if I really wanted to tell him what happened.

"Chrissy?"

Nibbling on the corner on my lower lip, I told him, "I stabbed Sapphire."

Roughly yanking me by the forearm, He pulled me up onto the front porch and took me into the house. "You did what!"

"I stabbed her."

Releasing me, he brushed his hand across his waves. "Did anyone see you do it?"

"I-I don't think so." I was in such a rush that I didn't pay attention to anything else. I didn't recall seeing anyone out there other than her.

"Is she dead?"

"I don't know."

"What the fuck you mean you don't know? How come you didn't call me for help?"

"Why would I call you?" My face frowned up. Thugga was acting as if we were best of friends or something. I was only dealing with him because we both had a mutual interest—to make Kon pay. I somewhat didn't even trust his ass. He never told me exactly how he was going to make Kon pay. His intentions probably weren't the fucking best, so I needed to keep a damn eye on him for the most part.

"I could have helped you get rid of the body, so you wouldn't have to worry about getting caught. You left her somewhere—"

"In a parking lot," I added, shifting my eyes to the floor.

"In a parking lot... anyone could find her, and you don't even know if she's fucking dead. If she's still alive, she can easily wake up and tell the police what you did."

Sweat beads formed on my forehead. Either way, I was fucked. I hadn't thought about all of that when I went there. The only thing on my mind was the fact that the bitch was pregnant by my man and thought she was about to bring a child into the fucking world with him. I needed her ass out of the got damn picture and that was what fucking drove me to find her ass.

I went to extreme lengths to get a hold of her. Since I didn't know where to find her, I broke into her office and looked at her calendar to see exactly where she was. If she told the police what happened, it was a chance that I could go to jail for burglary and attempted murder. No way I was about to lose Stormie for the rest of my life.

"Do you think that I should go back there and see if she's still there?" My gaze met his again.

"Are you crazy?"

"I don't know what to do!" I tossed my hands into the air and plopped down on his leather sectional. The shit wasn't my style. I hated leather anything, but that was none of my business. I didn't have to be the one who lived there.

"You take your ass back there and you're bound to be walking right into getting your ass arrested." He slipped his phone out of his pocket and I observed as his fingers swiftly went across the keyboard. "I'ma send someone over there to check it out. What's the name of the building?"

"You know that building downtown where everyone be throwing all those parties at?"

"I'm not from here, shorty, so you gon' have to tell me what you're talking about."

"*Reign.*"

"Someone is on their way to check the shit out. In the meantime, you mind telling me why you stabbed her in the first place?" Treading over to the couch, he took the empty seat alongside me and I tucked my hair back behind my ear. I didn't want to go into detail with him about that. He was only just going to look at me crazy, thinking I was fucking insane. I mean, who wouldn't? I was still trying my best to hold on to a man that clearly made it known on several occasions that he wanted nothing else to do with my ass. My heart just wouldn't let him go.

Kon and I had too much fucking history together. You'd think that our history would make our bond unbreakable, but it didn't. He allowed some bitch off the fucking street to come in and break us apart.

"You're going to think it's stupid."

Lowering my head, I fiddled with my fingers.

Hooking me by the chin, he lifted my face and turned it to where I was facing him. "Try me."

"I found out she was pregnant."

"And you're still stuck on Kon?"

"I've been with him for nine years." Tears shimmered in my eyes. Never in a million years did I ever think I'd be so stuck on a man that I'd go to that sort of length to get him back. I wasn't a murderer, but the love I had for that man caused me to do some crazy ass things.

"Maybe you two just grew apart."

"Never!" That was something I wasn't willing to accept.

"It happens sometimes, Chrissy. There's nothing you can do about it, but move on."

"But I don't want to." I snatched away from him and gazed into space.

He pulled my face back toward his and said, "You deserve better than that."

"And what's better? He's really all I know."

"Stick with me and you'll find out."

Was he saying that he wanted to be with me? I was confused. We were only supposed to be getting Kon back, not trying to make something out of this situationship. It didn't even feel right to think of him in that way.

He glanced down at his phone and he fell silent.

"What's wrong?"

His gaze met mine again and he said, "She's not there."

"What!" I bolted to my feet and my heart dropped to the pit of my stomach. "I'm gonna go to jail."

"Calm down, Chrissy. Just because she wasn't there, doesn't mean that you're going to jail. Maybe you're lucky enough for her to be dead, that way she wouldn't be able to tell anyone that you did it."

"Hopefully, or else I could lose my daughter."

Thugga rose to his feet and caught me by the shoulders, staring deep into my eyes. "You're not going to lose your daughter if I have anything to do with it. It just means that we must get a move on getting Kon. Once he's out of the picture, he won't be able to take her away from you."

"But what if Sapphire goes to the police?"

"You were here with me all night, right? It's her word against yours."

I was beginning to like Thugga already.

"Thank you."

Releasing me, he tread toward the dining room that was connected to the living room and disappeared. "You hungry!" he shouted back, and I exhaled. I could finally breathe again, knowing that everything was going to be okay.

"Starving."

Konfidence "Ken" White

I had been fucking blowing Blessed's phone up to see how the shipment went. I hadn't heard anything else from him after he called me that morning to say that he was going to pick up Don and check the shipment out. Don hadn't been answering the phone either and the shit had me fucking worried that something had happened to them. I hadn't heard anything from my ears on the street, so I knew I had to go out and search for answers my damn self.

If I wasn't busy with Stormie that morning, then I would have been able to accompany him on the mission and wouldn't be worried that something had gone wrong. It had to have been if neither one of them were answering the fucking phone.

I rode by the trap on Coral Gate Drive and no one was there. Sitting on the side of the road, I sent out a 911 message searching for a location on that bitch Stephanie that Blessed had been associating with. I knew that someone was bound to send back the ho's location with the price tag that was attached to the motherfucker's head. Blessed should have gave me more details about that got damn shipment or at least the fucking route then I could have gone by there to see what the fuck was going on. He was too fucking anxious to get a hold of Thugga. I was eager as hell too, but with how dangerous shit was, I wouldn't have been out there half-stepping and shit to get myself fucked up.

The more time that passed, the more I fucking panicked. Bad thoughts tried to seep its way into my fucking mind. My phone finally dinged, and someone had sent me a text with the whereabouts of Stephanie. I wasted no time placing the car in drive and sped to the other side of town.

I didn't know a damn thing about that bitch, but her name. Shit, I didn't even know what she looked like. I could have easily passed her on the street and wouldn't even fucking know it. I hated to admit that I was slipping when it came to our business. With everything that I had going on with Chrissy, Stormie, and Sapphire, my mind had been elsewhere. I guess it was safe to say that I needed to get a fucking handle on my shit.

Pulling into *Magnolia's Soul food* restaurant, I quickly parked my car, grabbed my gun from my waistline and jumped out. It may have seemed like I was taking shit entirely too fucking far, but most of the time, drastit measures always got the fucking job done.

Entering the building, I stopped at the door and noticed that it was damn near full of people. No way I was going to be able to find that Stephanie bitch without a hassle. People were talking and laughing with so much fucking commotion going on that I damn near lost my mind.

Pow!

Before I knew it, I let off one round into the ceiling and all eyes fell on me.

"Glad I got your attention. I just need one person and I'll be out of here."

"Hope you know that you're going to be paying for the damages to my ceiling or else I'm calling the cops," an older woman said, nearing me. Anyone else, they probably would have run off if a fool came into their restaurant and shot into their ceiling, but not her. From the mug on her face and the tone of her voice, I could tell that she was probably from the hood herself.

"Once you all give me who I came here for, I'll give you whatever for that ceiling."

"How are we supposed to know who you came for when you came in here shooting instead of asking questions?"

"I'm looking for someone name Stephanie."

"Which one is she?"

"I don't know."

She snickered and gazed out at the other people sitting in her restaurant with wide eyes, trying to figure out what was going to happen next. "You come in here looking for a girl and don't know what she looks like."

"Let's just say that she's a mutual friend." A smirk passed my lips.

"Okay." Shrugging, she said, "Which one of you is Stephanie?"

No one answered and I knew that was probably because they were scared shitless and they had the fucking right to be. If she didn't step forward, there were going to be consequences. That motherfucker was wasting both of our got damn time. Turning back to me, she asked, "Are you sure she's supposed to be here?"

"Positive." I eyed the people sitting before me, trying to see if I could sniff her ass out. I noticed a chick sitting in the back of the restaurant with two other girls. Her eyes shied away from me when she realized I was looking in her direction. "Think I just found her."

Nearing the back of the restaurant, I stopped directly at their table and slammed my strap down on it. All three of them jumped and gasped, but Stephanie squeezed her eyes shut. She knew something about Blessed, the shit was written all over her fucking face.

"You're Stephanie?"

"No!" she quickly shouted as if that was going to make me believe her.

"Why you won't look me in the fucking eyes then?"

Squeezing her eyes shut, she took a deep breath and glanced up at me. They watered which gave her ass away even more. Gripping her by the arm, I yanked her from the booth and dragged her toward the door.

"Let go of me! Help!" she screamed, staring back at the other people in the restaurant, but they all looked away including her so-called friends. I pulled her out the door and slammed her up against the brick wall.

"Where's my money for the ceiling?" the woman from the restaurant asked me with her hand out.

"Are you serious?" I frowned at her.

"Damn right; my money..." Her fingers wiggled as she waited for me to hand over the money I promised her.

Holding Stephanie with one hand, I shoved the other into my pocket and pulled out a wad of cash, slamming it down into her palm. "Here."

"Don't ever bring your ass back," she said and went back into the building.

I turned my attention back to Stephanie. Tears shimmered in her eyes. She probably figured her life was coming to an end. If she hadn't fucked over Blessed and Don, then she wouldn't have a damn thing to worry about.

"Where the fuck is Blessed and Don?"

"I don't know what you're talking about."

"You really gon' stand there and lie to my motherfucking face?" I shoved the gun into the side of her fucking dome. "Now, I'm gon' ask you again... where the fuck is Blessed and Don." Her lips parted and I suddenly stopped her. "If I were you, I'd think before speaking. If your answer isn't shit I wanna hear, I'ma send a bullet crashing through your motherfucking skull."

She stood there silently gazing into my eyes with her

watery ones. I pressed the gun deeper into her skull. "Okay! Okay!" She swallowed so hard that I could hear it. "They went to the shipment. It happened this morning, so I'm quite sure Blessed walked into more than he was bargaining for."

"Bitch, you set him up?"

"No!" she swiftly answered.

"What the fuck happened then? They never made it back and I haven't heard anything from them."

"I don't know."

"What was the shipment route?... Matter of fact..." Roughly gripping her by the arm, I snatched her away from the wall and pulled her in the direction of my car. "You're gonna fucking show me."

"I can't go anywhere with you. If Thugga got word that—"

"Fuck Thugga!" I barked, spit flying from my lips. "You got Blessed into some bullshit and you gon' help me get him out of it." Stopping in my tracks, I slung her around to where she faced me. "If I get a fucking hunch that you're up to some bullshit, I'm gon' rock yo' shit," I said, shoving her toward the car. "Get in the motherfucking car."

Taking one glance at me, she grabbed the door handle and slid into the seat. Rounding the car, I climbed in alongside her and pulled out of the parking lot. She was silent at first, making me think I was really going to have to kill her stupid ass for not telling me how to find Blessed and Don until she started throwing out directions.

Following them precisely, she brought me to this narrow street where I spotted Blessed's car parked on the side of the road. Yellow tape was tied to the streetlights on either side of the street. I slammed down on brakes and faced Stephanie, shoving my gun into her face. "I don't know what happened!" She shouted, tossing her hands into the air.

"You better figure the fuck out what happened before your fucking brains is splattered all over that got damn window behind you.

With trembling hands, she reached into her pocket and pulled out her cell phone. I observed as her fingertips swiftly dialed a number and she placed the phone up to her ear. My heart pounded rapidly in my chest, thinking that Blessed had been fucking killed. I couldn't help but feel like the shit was my got damn fault because I wasn't in fucking place.

"Fuck!" I barked, punching the steering wheel and she jumped.

Clearing her throat, she said, "Hey, Thugga. When you want me to meet you at the warehouse to help with the shipment?"

I mouthed, "Put it on speaker." Because I didn't trust the bitch. If she indeed had set Blessed and Don up, I wasn't about to give her the fucking opportunity to do me the same got damn way.

"You got a lot of fucking guts calling my mother fucking phone. I don't need you to help me with shit. You—"

"Wait, what?" Her brows furrowed.

"Your traitor ass been fucking with that nigga Blessed. Bet you thought I didn't got damn know. You set my shit up this morning, but yo' 'lil boyfriend didn't see that shit coming." Her eyes locked with mine and I waved the gun in her face.

"What did you do?"

"I sent that motherfucker to meet his got damn maker."

My teeth clenched when he said that. All I could think about was putting him and her ass six fucking feet under.

"I—"

"Save the bullshit ass lies, Step. Yo' ass dead when I get a hold of your ass." The call ended and her watery eyes landed on me.

"I swear I didn't know he knew. If I did, I wouldn't have ever sent Blessed into that ambush."

Wham!

My gun went straight across her fucking face, knocking her unconscious. Clutching the steering wheel, I gazed at Blessed's car and moisture filled my eyes. It took everything in me not to place a hot one in that bitch's skull.

My phone rang and I pulled it from the cup holder. An unknown number flashed across the screen. I thought about not answering the shit, but I picked up anyway.

"Who the hell is this?" My blood boiled and I turned around on the street.

"Is this Konfidence White?" The female's voice asked.

"I asked who the fuck this is..." This bitch was pissing me the fuck off calling me by my government and shit. Not too many people knew my real name, so I really wanted to know who the fuck she was calling my got damn phone.

"Uh, this is Tracy at Mercy Hospital. I'm calling you because a Mr. Blessed had you down as his emergency contact. He—"

"He's okay? He's at the hospital?" I quickly cut her off, glancing over at Stephanie as I mashed the gas and zoomed through traffic. I don't know why I believed that nigga Thugga when he said he killed Blessed. Why would a nigga of his so-called caliber lie about something like that unless he assumed he was dead when they left him lying in the street? Thankfully, someone found him, and he was all right... at least that was what I was assuming if she was on my phone.

"He's fine. He just got out of surgery and was placed into recovery. I just wanted to give someone a call and let them know he was here."

"Okay. I'm on my way."

Ending the call, I dropped my phone into my lap and raced

to the hospital. Pulling into the parking lot, I quickly jumped from the car, leaving it sitting at the emergency entrance. I was in such a fucking hurry to make sure Blessed was okay that I forgot to do something with that bitch Stephanie. She was just going to have to wait.

Stopping at the nurse's station, I said, "I received a call about my brother Blessed Thomas." I watched as she typed away on her computer in search of his name. My heart skipped beats in my chest not knowing what she was going to say. "I received a call saying he was in recovery. Is he out?"

Her eyes briefly cut to me, then returned to her screen. "They moved him to room 234." I didn't even give her a chance to say anything else before I shot to the elevator.

I didn't know where the hell Don was, but at least I knew that Blessed was all right. If he was up to it, I was going to ask him what the hell happened with the shipment for clarity. I know Thugga tried to kill him, but he made it out if there alive somehow.

Stopping in front of his door, I took a deep breath and pushed it in. Blessed lay there, in bed, hooked up to machines. They beeped as I made my way into the room and over to the side of his bed. I hated seeing my nigga lay there like that, but I'd rather he be in a hospital bed than a fucking casket.

"Damn, I should have been there," I said, gazing down at him. He must have heard my voice because his eyes fluttered open.

"Kon?" His voice was low and raspy.

"Yeah, nigga, its me."

He pointed at the cup of water sitting on the table next to his bed, so I grabbed it and handed it over to him. I watched as he took a sip and lifted the bed up to see better.

"How the fuck I let this shit happen?" He questioned me and I was confused as fuck.

"What are you talking about? How were you supposed to know that Thugga was going to try and take you out?" If you asked me, all this shit was that hoe Stephanie's fault. She should have done better research before sending them in there. Lucky for her, Blessed was still motherfucking breathing and I didn't have to place a got damn bullet in her ass. The shit was tempting as fuck though.

"I'm not talking about that."

"What are you talking 'bout then?"

"Don... that nigga working with Thugga."

"You sure?"

"Hell yeah. That motherfucker the one that put me in here."

I couldn't believe the shit I was hearing. Out of all the shit that we'd done for the little nigga, and for him to turn his fucking back on us like that was fucked up. I found that nigga at his lowest fucking point and put him on in the motherfucking game and he fucking repaid me by going out there dealing with the got damn enemy. Out of all people that I would have thought would have switched up on my ass... Don was far from the list, but I guess you never know what a motherfucker had up their got damn sleeve, especially when money was involved. Money was the only reason I could think that Don would change on us. Greed was a powerful thing.

"Wait 'til I get my hands on that motherfucker," I said, plopping down in the sectional next to his bed. My mind was all over the fucking place. Not only did I have to place that motherfucker Thugga six feet under, I had to bury one of my most loyalist niggas from over the years. The shit just wasn't sitting right with my soul.

"I wanna be the one to handle his bitch ass. That nigga really thought he was doing something when he shot me, but little do he fucking know, all he did was sign his own got damn death sentence." I noted the murder in Blessed's eyes. He wanted to get his hands on Don badly. I didn't blame him. Don was like a little brother to him in a way. He dealt with him way more than I did and basically brought him in under his wing. At the time that Don came into the picture, I'd just had Stormie and didn't really have time to deal with him, so Blessed trained him and really taught him everything he knew excluding the traitor part. That shit had to have already been in his fucking blood.

"We'll get him." Pulling my phone from my pocket, I realized how late it was and that I had a missed call from an unknown number. I figured that the nurse was trying to call me from another number to see if I made it to check on Blessed. Ignoring it, I slipped the phone back into my pocket and rose to my feet.

"I gotta get going. I haven't talked to Sapphire since earlier and now that I know you're okay, I'ma take my ass on to the house before she tries to rip me a new ass hole." I chuckled. She had an event earlier that's why I didn't want to bother her with the issue about Blessed, but judging by the time, I knew she should have made it back home.

"Let me know if you get anything on Don."

"Will do."

Blessed was eager to get his hands on Don's ass and honestly, I didn't really blame him. I wasn't sure where that motherfucker was, but I was sure he was laying low somewhere after the bullshit he pulled. One thing was for sure, he wasn't going to show his face at the trap again. If he did, he was one stupid ass motherfucker and wanted to be fucking dealt with. In case he was that fucking stupid, I was going to put eyes on the house.

My fingers swiftly went across my keyboard texting Rod as I made my way toward the elevator. He was another one of my lieutenants that worked at another trap across town. Since I could no longer trust Don, I had to entrust him to get the fucking job done.

Exiting the building, I scrubbed my hand across my mouth,

feeling the weight of the world release from my shoulders. I still wasn't in the fucking clear and wasn't going to be until I handled Don and Thugga for fucking good.

My eyes locked on Stephanie as she took a long toke from a cigarette. She had a bruise on her face right underneath her left eye, but that's what the fuck she got. She should have fucking spoke up about the damn situation. I felt like she knew something wasn't right that's why she was at that got damn restaurant and not the fucking warehouse with Thugga.

"Thought you would have been gone by now," I said, and she jumped.

"You scared me," she replied with the cigarette dangling from her lips. I hated a chick that smoked. That shit wasn't sexy to me. They probably could get away with smoking weed, but not no got damn cigarettes. Tossing it to the ground, she stepped on it and said, "Where was I going to go? Thugga has it out for my fucking head."

"And you're telling me this because..." I had nothing to do with what the fuck she had going on. I got out of her what I needed, and she served no other purpose for me. Rounding my car, I grabbed the handle and she suddenly stopped me.

"You have to help me."

"Why the fuck would I do that?"

"'Cause I helped you."

"Wrong fucking answer." I yanked the door open and went to climb into the car.

"I can be beneficial to you!"

This motherfucker would say anything to not get left for dead.

Chuckling, I replied, "And what makes you think that?"

"I can help you get Thugga."

"Do you really think he'd be stupid enough to operate the

same after he knows that you were working with Blessed?" I saw no point in keeping her around. If she switched up on Thugga... I was positive that she'd do me the same way granted the opportunity.

"Please... you have to help me." Tears glistened in her eyes, but that shit wasn't going to fucking work on me. I'd stared crying people in the eyes before and still pulled the trigger on their ass. "If I can't help you get Thugga, then you can place a bullet in me yourself."

"F—" Just as I was about to respond to her, I noticed Sa'nai running across the parking lot. I assumed that she probably got word about Blessed and wanted to come and check on him. It shocked me that they were even still fucking around. Him messing with one woman just wasn't him.

Her eyes locked on me and she stormed over in my direction with the meanest mug she could muster up resting on her face.

"Really Kon!" She shouted and I had the slightest clue as to what she was talking about.

"What?"

"You're out here talking to this bitch when you should be inside!" Her hands tossed in the air as she spoke. From her facial expression, I could tell she was furious as hell.

"I just came from in there. You need to chill the fuck out; it's not even what you think."

"What is it then? Sapphire is in there fighting for her got damn life... hers and your fucking baby and you're out here talking to the next bitch."

My mind tried to process the shit she just said. I eased away from the car, nearing her. "What the fuck did you just say?"

Folding her arms over her chest, she shifted all her weight to her right side and frowned. "You heard what the fuck I said."

"Sapphire isn't in there. She's at home."

"No, she's not. She never made it there. Wanna know how come I know?" I didn't respond just eyed her and she continued. "I got a call from Sasha saying that she found her lying in the fucking parking lot bleeding to death. Wonder who tried to kill her?" Her face twisted up as she stared at me as if I had some shit to do with it.

"The fuck you trying to say?"

I wanted her to say the wrong shit, so I could knock her the fuck out.

"All I'm saying is that none of this shit would have happened if she hadn't started fucking with you. Don't think I don't know about that crazy bitch Chrissy threatening her and shit. Yeah, she told me all about that shit. And if I find out she had something to do with this, you gon' be buying a black dress to bury her ass in."

"Trust me, if she had something to do with this shit, you won't even make it to kill her ass 'cause I'm gon' beat you to the shit."

Shutting my car door, I tread back into the hospital with Sa'nai and Stephanie right on my heels. Could this day possibly get any fucking worse?

Sa'nai Gates

I stood there chewing on the inside of my jaw, fiddling with my fingers, debating on what I wanted to do. I wanted to go over there and strangle Kon's ass to death. All this shit was his fucking fault and he sat there as if he'd done nothing wrong. Then the fucking nerve of him to still have that bitch there with him. Heat coursed through my veins. Both of those motherfuckers were wrong, but there wasn't shit I could do about it.

All I could think about was what if Sapphire had died when I received that phone call from Sasha. My heart dropped to the pit of my stomach. Sapphire was really all I had left, and I didn't want to see anything happen to her. It killed me standing down there like a sitting duck waiting for someone to come to me with some news.

"What the fuck are you looking at?" I asked the bitch sitting with Kon with a frown. I noticed how she kept eyeing me and shit as if she had something to say. If she said anything wrong, I was bound to go over there and place her ass in one of those fucking hospital beds.

Her head quickly snapped in the other direction. Kon rose to his feet and neared me. If he knew what was best for him, he would have stayed the fuck away from me. I still said that scary ass bitch baby mama of his was the one that did this shit, and when I got my hands on her ass, it was over.

"Save it Kon; I don't even wanna hear it."

"All I was 'bout to say was that maybe you should go up there and see Blessed. Maybe that'll take your mind off of shit for a while. Knowing these motherfuckers, they gon' take forever to let someone know something."

"You're just tryna get rid of me, so you can be alone with that bitch." My eyes darted in her direction and she shifted in her seat. I was pissed with his ass like I was the one fucking him.

"That shit ain't even what you think. I used her to find Blessed."

"He's fucking her!" My eyes grew wide as saucers. That gave me even more reason to go over there and fuck that bitch up. I charged toward her and he caught me by the waist.

"She's not fucking either of us. If anything, she's the reason he's in here in the first place."

"Why the fuck you holding me then! Let me go over there and rearrange that bitch's face!" I squirmed in his arms, but he didn't release me.

"I can't let you do that."

"Why the fuck not?" My entire body froze. He had me feeling like he wasn't telling me something.

"I need her. After I'm done with her, you can do whatever you want with her ass."

"You don't have to tell me twice."

He released me and I brushed the invisible wrinkles out of my dress and sighed.

"I'm going to go check on Blessed. Let me know if they say anything about Sapphire." I didn't want to leave from down there without knowing what happened to her, but if I was to stay down there, it was just going to tempt me to dig my foot off in that hoe's ass.

Kon nodded and I strolled toward the elevator. I took one final look at her and stepped on. She was all in Kon's face and shit, probably mad that he said I could have my way with her ass when they were done. I couldn't wait to get my hands on her, but for now, I was going to go by and check on my man to make sure he was okay.

So much was weighing heavily on me. My man and best friend were both lying in the same hospital and everything pointed back to Kon. I knew they were up to some illegal shit that's why he wouldn't ever tell me where he was going. He always kept saying it was for my own protection, but it looked like to me, he needed to be the one being protected, not me.

Stopping in front of his door, I grabbed the knob and took a couple of breaths. I wasn't sure how I was going to react when I saw him lying in that bed or how he was going to look. That was the main reason why I hadn't been up there yet. Kon told me what room he was in when we first got into the hospital, but I was putting off going to see him. I hated seeing the people that I cared about down and out. It made me want to do whatever in my power to soothe them.

Pushing the door open, I stepped into the room and my eyes landed on him. He lay there sleeping peacefully as hell. I didn't even want to go further into the room and wake him. Sinking my teeth into my lower lip, I turned to leave quietly.

"Nai?" He called out my name, stopping me.

Freezing in place, I slowly turned back to face him. "I didn't try to wake you."

"Were you really about to sneak out of the room?"

"No," I lied with a grin and eased to the side of his bed.

"Yes, the hell you were."

"You were sleeping so peacefully."

"You think I didn't want to see you or something?"

"It's not that..."

"What is it then?" He gripped my hand and butterflies fluttered in my stomach.

"Nothing. How are you feeling?" I quickly changed the subject.

"I'm okay. How are you and my baby?"

I rubbed my stomach completely forgetting I was pregnant. "We're okay. Sapphire is here too. I think that bitch Chrissy stabbed her."

"Hell nah." He laughed that shit off and winced a little bit.

"Hell yeah. She been threatening Sapphire 'bout Kon. I don't see how someone could be that fucking dick whipped to try and kill someone over the shit."

"You mean to tell me that you wouldn't try to kill a bitch over this dick?"

"Hell no. Are you crazy?" A smile passed my lips and he yanked me down toward his face. Our lips meshed, and I felt like I was in heaven. I loved spending time with Blessed and to know that we were about to bring a baby into this world together was unbelievable.

His phone vibrated on the table next to his bed and I grabbed it, handing it over to him. He glanced down at the screen and brought his gaze back to mine.

"Kon said that they placed Sapphire on a room. Room 348."

I nibbled on the corner of my lower lip. I was excited to know that Sapphire was doing well, but I was still scared to go into the room with her. According to Sasha, she was stabbed in the stomach and I was terrified to know how the baby was doing. I know she didn't want it in the first place, but if Chrissy has taken that baby away from her, I felt sorry for her. Sapphire was already a fucking firecracker with everyone, but when she was pissed the fuck off, it was like starting World War 3. Anybody could fucking get it.

"You alright?" Blessed asked, bringing me from my

thoughts.

"I just don't know how Sapphire is going to react."

"Go check on her. I'll be right here when you get back."

"I know; it's not like you can go anywhere." I snickered and pecked him on the lips. "I'll be right back."

Treading out of the room, I headed to the elevator praying that Kon got rid of that hoe before he went into the room to see Sapphire. She already had enough going on, she didn't need to get her pressure up thinking he was fucking off on her and shit.

Getting off on her floor, I followed the signs to Sapphire's room. The door was wide open, so I didn't have to knock. Kon stood at the side of her bed talking to her when I entered. Sapphire's eyes landed on me and the conversation stopped.

"Sa'nai." Tears formed in her eyes and my heart crushed into tiny millions of pieces. My best friend was laying there hurting and there was nothing I could do about it.

"I was so worried 'bout you!" Rushing into the room, I flew straight into her arms and wept. Sapphire's tears dripped on my shoulder like raindrops.

"I lost my baby," she cried, and I felt so bad for her.

"It's okay as long as you're alright."

"I tried to tell her that," Kon interrupted. I wanted to say that no one was fucking talking to him, but I opted out of it, not wanting to start an argument in front of her. He already knew I was pissed the fuck off with him, so I didn't have to make it known.

"Who did this to you?" I questioned her.

"I was just 'bout to get around to asking her that." I shot Kon daggers. I had a gut feeling of who had done it, but I wanted her to say it to be sure.

"It was Chrissy." Her eyes darted to Kon. "Why did you tell

her I was pregnant?"

"See, I knew this shit was your fucking fault!" I shoved him hard in the chest and he stumbled a little bit.

"You need to calm the fuck down." He mugged me, but I didn't give a fuck. Sapphire could have died from that shit.

"And you need to put a leash on that bitch! What if she would have killed her!" All I saw was fucking red and I wanted to go out there and hunt that hoe down and give her exactly what the fuck she deserved. Chrissy was running around here playing a dangerous fucking game. She was lucky I wasn't with Sapphire or else they would have been carrying her away in a got damn body bag. That bitch definitely had it coming if I ran into her on the street.

"I'ma deal with her," he said, brushing his hand across his waves.

"Yeah, you fucking better." I turned my attention back to Sapphire. She gazed into space, rubbing her hand on her stomach. She may have told me that she didn't want that baby, but now that it was no longer an option, I think she was second guessing it. "You okay?" I asked her, bringing her back to reality.

"I will be." She flashed me a fake smile.

I sat there with her for a little while longer just lost in my thoughts. Kon had been dipped on us. He probably went to take that bitch somewhere. I thanked God he wasn't stupid enough to bring her into the room with him.

Glancing over at Sapphire, she was fast asleep, so I got up and eased out of the room to go check on Blessed. It had been a few hours since I left him to go see her and I wanted to go back and talk to him.

As I entered his room, his nurse was in there checking his vitals, so I stood off to the side to wait until she was done.

"Is there anything I can get you?" She asked him, removing

the pressure cuff.

"I'm good right now," he replied.

"Okay. Just call me if you need me." She left out of the room shutting the door behind her and I eased over to his bed. A smile passed his lips when his gaze met mine.

"How is she?" He questioned pertaining to Sapphire.

"She's fine are the moment. I was right though... Chrissy was the one that stabbed her."

"Damn, that's fucked up. What did Kon day 'bout the shit?"

"Talking about he gon' handle it, but I'ma hunt that bitch down my damn self and put a bullet in her ass." I'd never shot anyone before, but if that meant that Sapphire was going to be safe, then I'd damn sure do it.

"You need to sit yo' ass down somewhere. You're not killing anyone. You're pregnant and I'm not letting anything happen to you or my baby."

I don't know why I thought he was going to be on my side with that. Either way, I was going to do what needs to be done to protect my best friend.

"It's alright for you to go out there and do stupid shit every day risking your fucking life, but when I want to do something that actually means something, you got something to say."

"That's not the same thing and you fucking know it."

"I'm not about to sit here and go back and forth with you 'bout this." Tossing my hands into the air, I tread to the door.

"So, you get mad 'cause I won't let you do something stupid as fuck, you want to dip on a nigga."

I rushed back over to the bed, nostrils flaring. "I don't know shit 'bout Kon. He claims he gon' take care of the shit, but that's his baby mama. It's not gon' be much he gon' do to her ass. That bitch needs to be handled and I mean where she can't hurt anyone ever again."

Never in my life has murder ever been on my mind, but it was all I could fucking think about at the moment.

"But you know me and I'm gon' make sure she's dealt with accordingly."

"Yeah, whatever. I'm going back to Sapphire's room." Without saying another word, I left out of there, shutting the door behind me. Blessed wanted to talk shit or whatever, but I was going to hunt that bitch Chrissy down and make her ass pay if it was the last fucking thing I did.

Sapphire Snow

A week later...

I t had been an entire week since I made it back home from the hospital. Shit was different. I felt different. My mind was so fucked up that I decided I needed to take some time from work. This was the first time ever that I'd gone this long without going into the office or working from my laptop.

After that shit happened with Chrissy, I no longer felt safe. It was a good thing that Kon had moved me in with him when he did. At least I knew that crazy bitch didn't know how to find me for the moment.

Kon had been searching for her ass to talk to her. I felt as if he needed to do more than fucking talking. That bitch tried to fucking kill me and if she knew I was still alive, there's no telling if she was going to try and come back to finish the damn job.

Kon was worried as well. He was so fucking worried that he didn't want me leaving the house, but I couldn't hide from her ass forever. That shit just wasn't in me. My pride wouldn't allow me to. Once I was done processing what happened to me, I was sure I was going to be able to face that bitch on my own. She may have thought she was getting away with something, but she was wrong.

I'm not going to lie. When I first found out that Kon even called and told her I was pregnant, I was pissed the fuck off. She didn't need to know my fucking business like that. I felt that if she hadn't known, then I wouldn't have lost my baby. I was still kind of complexed about the entire situation. She took away my right to keep or have the baby, and that shit was fucked up.

I swirled my coffee in my mug, gazing into space. My mind was all over the place and normally when I got like that, I'd throw myself into work. Since I wasn't working at the moment, I wasn't sure what the hell I was going to do.

"Are you okay?" Stormie asked me, bringing me from my thoughts. I flashed her a false smile. It was hard to be calm around her knowing that her mother took my child away from me and tried to take my fucking life. Some might have taken the shit out on her, but she was just a child and has nothing to do with her dumb ass mother's actions.

"Yes, I'm okay, sweetie." I lied to her because I didn't want to have to try to explain to her why I was upset. Even though Chrissy tried to kill me, I didn't want to have to paint that picture for her child and destroy the imagine she held of her mother. Another bitch probably would have done the shit out of spite, but I was made different.

"You sure? You've been standing there with that same cup for the last thirty minutes."

"I'm alright." Nearing her, I patted her on the shoulder and flashed her another one of my famous fake ass smiles. "I just have a lot on my mind, that's all."

"Okay," was all she said before bouncing off.

The doorbell chimes and I slipped the cup onto the island and left out of the kitchen. I wasn't sure who it was because I wasn't expecting anyone. Opening the door, I was greeted with Sa'nai's welcoming smile. Lifting her hands, she greeted me with a takeout bag and drinks.

"I thought that maybe you could use some company."

Nodding my head, I stepped to the side and allowed her inside. Almost every day all day, she was blowing my phone up to check on me. No matter how much I told her that I was alright, she didn't believe me. She had to understand that I was strong as fuck and was going to make it through this bullshit with my head held high. It may take a while for me to get to that point, but I was going to get there.

I followed her into the family room, and she placed the food down on the coffee table, taking a seat on the sectional.

I gently sat down alongside her and said, "I almost told Stormie what her mama did."

"I'm glad you didn't. Kon probably would kill your ass. Speaking of that nigga, has he found that bitch yet?" That was her main question every day. I don't know why she was so anxious for him to find Chrissy.

Ever since he found out that Chrissy tried to kill me, he had been searching high and low for her ass. It was like she disappeared off the face of the fucking earth. Even her fucking phone was disconnected. She was dumb as fuck because basically, she was letting it be known that she was guilty. I don't see how she shut her own child out like that.

The first couple of days, Stormie asked about her mother because she was supposed to come and pick her up, but after that, it was as if she was no longer relevant. Everything about Chrissy was bitch made. I could tell that from the moment I met her. If she was bold enough to try and kill someone, then she should have been fucking bold enough to suffer the consequences.

"No, he hasn't found her, but you'd be the first to know if he had."

"I just wanna beat the bitch's ass and maybe put her in the fucking ground for what she fucking did to you." I loved how she rode for me. Sa'nai had always been protective of me since we were younger and vice versa.

"I understand that you love me and all, but I'm not about to sit by and let you kill that girl and throw your life away. You got too much going for yourself. Let Kon handle the shit." I couldn't believe I was saying that. A normal person would have gone to the fucking police behind that shit. They had visited me in the hospital, but I told them I didn't know who stabbed me. Kon wanted to be the one to take care of the situation, so I was going to let him.

"Why all y'all have to suck the fun out of everything." Pouting, she folded her arms over her chest, and I opened the bag to see what she brought me.

"I'm just trying to look out for you."

"And I'm trying to look out for you, but all of y'all tripping and shit."

"You're not a killer, Sa'nai. Just leave the shit to Kon and Blessed."

I didn't like the idea of having them do anything either, but I knew that was their lifestyle and there was nothing I could do to change that. Deep down, I had a feeling that if the situation presented itself, Kon wasn't going to kill Chrissy. They had too much fucking history together. If he didn't do something with her ass, then I was just going to have to go to someone that would—the police.

Ignoring me, she grabbed her food and opened the to-go plate. "I'm serious, Sa'nai. Leave the shit up to them."

"I hear you." Rolling her eyes, she dug into her food. I don't know why, but I had a feeling she wasn't going to fucking listen to me.

∞∞∞

Sa'nai had long left the house and I was stuck there with Stormie, trying my best to avoid her. No matter how much I told her that I was fine, she didn't believe me. She and I had grown close since I'd been dealing with Kon. I wouldn't say that I looked at her as a daughter just yet, but close enough.

Distancing myself from Stormie was for two reasons: one, I didn't want to slip up and say the wrong thing around her... two, it made me wonder how Kon's and my child would have looked and the shit was painful.

Everyone kept telling me that I was young and could have another child. That I should be thankful I was still living, but they weren't the one who had their baby taken away from them. It was one thing to think about not having it or handing it over to someone that was more fit than me, but to have someone take that choice away from you... that was a different kind of pain.

Tears formed in my eyes as I sat there in the dark with a million things on my mind. If I didn't get my shit together and soon, I was going to fucking lose my got damn mind.

The door opened and the light from the hallway damn near blinded me. I squeezed my eyes shut, shielding my face with my hand.

"Why you sitting in the dark?" Kon questioned me and I peeked at him with one eye open. He and I hadn't really been on the best of terms lately. I looked at it as being his fault that I was in the hospital and almost died. He should have been done something with that bitch when I told him she was calling my got damn office and threatening me. If he had put a fucking leash on her ass then, I'd still have my fucking baby.

Ignoring him, I turned over in bed, facing the wall. I would have gone back to my house to stay away from him, but I had sold it when he asked me to move in with him. Plus, I knew that he was just going to hunt me down, especially after he already made it known he didn't want me leaving the house alone until he found Chrissy.

If that bitch knew what was fucking best for her ass, she'd stay the fuck away from me. She may have caught me slipping that time, but I promise if she came anywhere near me again, I was going to put a bullet in her ass. That's right. After that incident, I took one of Kon's guns and had been keeping it nearby. No way I was going to give her the fucking opportunity to try to kill me again. It might just be her luck that she actually fucking succeeded.

"I know you're not still mad at me."

It had been a week and I had been treating Kon like shit. I could tell it bothered him from his facial expression, that's why I didn't want to look him in the face. If I had, I probably would have just given in.

"Sapphire?" The bed dipped down, and his hand touched my shoulder. I shrugged it off, squeezing my eyes a little bit tighter. "You can't keep walking around here like the shit my fault. I even apologized and didn't do anything wrong. You can't blame me for some shit my baby mama did."

Quickly turning over, I yelled, "I can! That bitch took my baby away from me and you were the one that brought that bitch into my life! If I had never—" My teeth sank into my lower lip, realizing what was about to escape from my lips.

"Never what?"

"Nothing." I shifted on the bed.

"No, gone say what you got to say." His eyes peered into mine and I felt even worse. I like Kon a lot and didn't want to say something out of anger I'd later regret, so I kept my mouth closed.

"You never what?... met me?"

I nibbled on the inside of my cheek. His eyes searched my face for answers, but I was quite sure he already had them.

"Is that really how you fucking feel?" I didn't respond just sat there, gazing at him. "Bet," was all he said before treading into the bathroom and slamming the door behind him.

Kon

Later that day...

"O ne... two... three," I said and Blessed kicked the door in. Me and Cam entered behind him with our guns drawn.

"Ain't nobody in here," Blessed announced from the kitchen.

"This bitch keeps sending us on dummy missions." Cam tucked his gun and flipped over the magazine on the coffee table.

"That's it, I'm fucking tired of this shit." Smoke seeped from my ears and I stormed out of the house and back to my car. For a fucking week straight, Stephanie had been giving us locations to hit in search of Thugga, but every single one of them was fucking empty. I don't know what type of fucking games she was trying to play, but that shit ended today.

"What the fuck are we gon' do now?" Blessed asked when he stepped out onto the porch. He was growing tired of doing the same shit every fucking day instead of being at home with his pregnant girl. I understood where he came from, but if he didn't put in the work, we weren't ever going to find that motherfucker and put an end to this bullshit. Sapphire, Stormie, and Sa'nai would never be safe.

It was already hard enough that Chrissy's ass was out there somewhere lurking in the fucking shadows. Out of all the fucking years I'd known that girl, I never thought she'd try to kill someone. I guess you never really know someone.

"We go back and deal with Stephanie's ass." I yanked the driver's side door open on my car and hopped inside. Blessed climbed into the truck with Cam and we pulled off.

Cam was Blessed's cousin. He was from Miami, but had been locked up for the last five years on a dope charge. The shit wasn't anything major, that's why he didn't get much time, but now that he was out, his sole purpose was to find Thugga's bitch ass and put a bullet in him.

Blessed and Cam grew up close as hell. Even though they were cousins, they looked at each other practically as brothers. That's why as soon as Cam heard about Blessed getting shot, he wasted no fucking time getting to us. That was fucking loyalty and it definitely was hard as fuck to come by these days.

I pulled up to the apartment I had Stephanie hiding out in. She claimed she feared going home because she knew it was only a matter of time before Thugga found her. Little did she know, the motherfucker she should have been fearing was me.

Hopping out of the car, I jogged up the flight of stairs and kicked the door in. I was so fucking angry that I forgot the fucking apartment was one of mine and not hers. I'd just have to get someone out here to fix the shit later.

Stephanie flew around the corner with wide eyes. She was wearing nothing, but a towel and it dropped to the floor.

"Got damn," Cam said from behind me.

"What the hell, Kon!" she shouted, bending down, picking up her towel. By the time she straightened her position, I was already in her face, gripping her by the fucking neck. Her body rammed against the wall behind her.

"I'm tired of your fucking bullshit." I ground my teeth so hard, the shit hurt.

"Wha-wha—" She could barely get a word out, that's how

tightly my hand crushed her fucking windpipes. She clawed at my hand, and all I wanted to do was squeeze her shit even more.

"Calm down, Kon. I'm sure she was just trying to help. Think about it… why would she fuck us over when she knows that we're the only ones that can keep her alive?" Blessed's hand rested on my shoulder and I brushed that shit off.

Shutting my eyes, I took a deep breath and released her. She gasped for air.

"He's right, Kon. I wouldn't do anything to piss you guys off. Thugga wants my fucking head and I'm sure he's going to try to get it at any cost. We both want the same thing."

Rubbing my hand up and down the nape of my nape, I replied, "Why the fuck every location you've given us has been bullshit?"

"'Cause Thugga is smart. He knows that I was working with Blessed to get him, so he switched everything up on us."

"What use are you to us then?" Cam questioned her, asking the exact question I had been asking myself the moment I decided to help her in the first place. I should have just sent her on about her fucking business, but I had some form of hope that she'd be some kind of assistance to us.

"I just have to see if I can get in touch with my old connects. I'm sure most of them are going to blackball me because of Thugga, but I'm sure I'd be able to turn at least one of them. Just give me some time," she said with pleading eyes.

"Your ass better do something or else you're going to be out there on your fucking own," I warned, treading to the doorway.

"What about the door?"

"I'll send someone by to fix it."

Scrubbing my hand across my mouth, I left out of the apartment and hopped back into my car. My mind was going a million miles a minute. After the shit that transpired with Sapphire earlier, I didn't even want to take my ass home to avoid getting into another argument with her ass.

It was crazy as fuck how she blamed me for the shit Chrissy had done. It wasn't like I placed a gun to her head and told her to go out and stab her. Did she not think I was just as angry as her? I just found out we were having a baby and Chrissy ripped that shit away from us like it was nothing. I was pissed the fuck off just as she was... if not even more.

Instead of going home, I decided to stop by Chrissy's mother's house to see if she had seen her. That shit was my last resort because I knew she didn't really fuck with her like that. Chrissy hated the very ground her mother walked on, but after the bullshit she pulled, I was sure she probably would have run to her.

I had tabs on her house to see if Chrissy would show up. No one had seen her, and I was growing impatient as hell waiting for her ass to resurface. If she was hiding, then she had to have known that I knew she was the one who tried to kill Sapphire. She had been neglecting Stormie since Sapphire and I had been together, but she hadn't gone this long without talking to her daughter. I was tired of having to lie to her about where the fuck her mother was. If she cared about her as much as she pretended to, then she'd come out or at least contact her to see how she was doing.

Pulling up to Lane's house, I sat on the side of the street for a moment to get a grip on my surroundings. Chad, the mother-fucker who I placed on Lane's house was parked a house down. When I climbed out of the car, he nodded at me and I trekked up to her front door.

I knew Lane was home because her Hyundai was parked in the driveway, plus, she didn't too much go any places besides work and Target. Fucking Target was that woman's favorite got damn store. Within a week, I learned her entire fucking life from Chad.

I thought about just kicking the fucking door in and demanding answers, but I decided to keep a low profile and just question her. If she didn't know where Chrissy was and she was to come by here, I didn't want to alert her by someone telling her I'd been by. People in Lane's neighborhood was nosey as fuck. I learned that shit from Chrissy when she used to tell me all about stories from when she was growing up. Everything she did, the entire neighborhood knew it before her mother did. That was one of the reasons why they didn't get along to this day. Lane looked at Chrissy as a fucking screw up and embarrassment.

Lane pulled the door open looking like an older version of Chrissy excluding the blonde hair. Those two were so much a fucking like, it was no wonder how come they kept bumping heads.

"What are you doing here, Kon?" she questioned me, propping her hand on her small hip.

"I need to talk to you."

"You've never seemed to *need* to talk to me before. Why now?"

"It's 'bout your daughter."

Sighing, she asked, "What has that child done now?" and stepped to the side to let me in.

My eyes roamed around the living room for any indication that Chrissy may have been there. I know Chad told me he hadn't seen her, but she could have easily snuck in when he wasn't paying attention or was on a break. I literally had that nigga sitting outside twenty-four-seven, waiting to see if she was going to show her face. He'd been ordering food and getting it delivered, using the bathroom outside, and taking cat naps in his car. Some may think the lengths I was taking was unnecessary, but I needed to get a hold of Chrissy before she tried to harm Sapphire again or became a danger to herself.

"Have you seen her lately?" I carefully studied Lane's face to see what her reaction was to my question to know if she was going to lie to me or not.

"No. Why you asked me that?"

"I really need to find her; it's important, so if you have seen her, I need you to tell me."

Nearing the couch, she took a seat and her gaze met mine. "I haven't seen Chrissy in I don't know how long. You know that child of mine barely comes around. I keep trying to get her to bring Stormie over, so I can see her, and she won't even do that." She shook her.

"I'll bring her by, so you can see her. Chrissy hasn't seen her in over a week. Probably longer than that."

"That's why you're looking for her?"

"No, I'm looking for her 'cause she killed my baby."

"What baby?" Her brow rose as she gazed at me. "She was pregnant again?"

"No, my girlfriend was."

"Wait." Her hand rose and eyes widened. "Since when did you two break up?"

"We been broke up because she couldn't stop fucking accusing me of cheating on her ass. I was sick and tired of her causing a damn scene."

"How did she kill your baby?"

"She stabbed my girlfriend in the stomach."

"Are you fucking serious?" From her facial expression, I could tell she was surprised to hear that.

"Yes."

"So, what do you plan on doing with her when you find her? You do realize that she's the mother to your other child, right?"

"I know that, and I hadn't thought that far." Sapphire wanted to know what I planned on doing with her as well, but I didn't want to end up saying the wrong thing. Either way, in this situation, someone was bound to get fucking hurt.

"Well, I don't know why you thought she would have been here."

"Just let me know if you see her or not."

"I doubt I will, but okay."

Even though those two didn't really get along, I doubted very seriously that she was going to let me know when or if Chrissy showed up. She didn't know what I planned on doing with her ass when she did, and she was still her mother. I'm positive she didn't want anything to happen to her.

Treading out of the house, I climbed back into my car and went home.

Chrissy

The next day...

I had been staying with Thugga until we figured out the situation about Sapphire. I had been keeping an eye on the news to see if she was dead, but hadn't heard anything. It was driving me fucking crazy not knowing if she was dead or not. So, fucking insane that I didn't want to leave the house and had turned my phone off.

Not wanting to depend on Thugga for cash, I decided to make a run to the store to grab a burner phone with the little cash I had in my wallet. I didn't even bother to use one of my cards because I had ghosted Kon and didn't want him to be able to track me down.

At first, I thought it was amazing having a man with it all and having him take care of me. I didn't know how restricted I was until I didn't want to be found.

My phone was off because that was another way, he'd be able to find me. I could have easily asked Thugga if I could use his phone, but I didn't want him to know who I was calling, let alone, let them be able to call back looking for me.

Exiting the corner store, I glanced around at my surroundings to make sure no one followed me there or had spotted me.

When the coast was clear, I hopped into Thugga's Jaguar and sat there for a moment. My heart pounded in my chest as my fingers dialed the number. I had always said I'd never dial this number again, especially not needing something.

I chewed on the inside of my jaw as the phone rang in my ear.

"Hello?" she answered, and I wanted to hang the phone up in her fucking face. "Hello?"

Squeezing my eyes shut, I took a deep breath. "Ma, it's me."

"Christina?" I sensed the shock in her voice.

"Yeah—"

"Where the hell have you been? How you just abandon Stormie like that? What the hell were you thinking?"

"You talked to Kon?" I should have known he was going to take it that far. If he was asking her about me, knowing I didn't fuck with her like that, he had to know that I killed Sapphire, right?

"He came by here yesterday asking me if I'd seen you."

"What did you say?"

"I told him no..."

"I need some money." I cut straight to the chase. I needed to beat Thugga back to the house before he found out that I took his car without his permission.

"Are you serious right now? You stop talking to me and think that if you call out of the blue asking for some money, you gon' get it?" She laughed and I wanted to slap the shit out of her through the fucking phone. That was the exact reason why I didn't fuck with that bitch in the first place. "And what's this bullshit I hear Kon say about you stabbing someone?"

I quickly glanced over my shoulder checking my surroundings as if someone could have heard what she said.

"Can you just meet me somewhere. I don't want to talk about this over the phone."

"No."

"Ma, please!" I was desperate as hell. If I couldn't get her to meet with me, I don't know what the hell I was going to do.

"Fine. Meet you where?"

"Meet me at this restaurant called *Crab Nation* in an hour."

"It's going to take me—"

"An hour, Ma!" I said and ended the call.

Taking the sim card out the back of the phone, I broke it in half and tossed it out of the window. I was really acting like a fucking criminal, but I had to be cautious if I didn't want to get caught by Kon or the fucking police. I quickly started the car and got the hell out of there.

It took me no time to make it to *Crab Nation*. When I got there, I frantically searched for my mother's car. I almost gave up after not seeing it, thinking she wasn't going to show up, but I saw her pull into the parking lot and park in the first spot she saw.

Climbing out of the car, she brushed her hair back behind her ear and glanced over her shoulder. She was giving off nervous vibes and had me feeling like something was up, but then again, she might have been nervous about being there to see me. She did know that I tried to kill someone. Maybe she no longer felt safe around me.

I waited a moment before getting out of the car and entering behind her. My heart thumped rapidly in my chest not knowing how this interaction with her was going to turn out.

I stood there in the doorway watching her from afar. She nervously tucked her hair back behind her ear. If being around me made her that fucking paranoid, I don't even know why she showed up in the first place. Taking a deep breath, I neared her table.

I never understood why people kept saying my mother and I looked identical. In my eyes, I didn't see the shit. Sure, we had the same bright complexion and length of hair, but that was because I'd cut mine that short. Other than that, we didn't look anything alike.

Stopping at the table, I gazed down into her eyes. She mugged me back and nodded toward the chair in front of her. Slowly, I pulled the seat out and sat down.

"Now are you going to tell me why Kon say you stabbed someone?" I knew she wasn't going to let that shit go. All she wanted was another reason to talk about me to her bitch ass friends.

"You haven't seen me in God knows when and the first thing you ask me is some bullshit Kon told you."

"Obviously, it's true if you've been hiding and calling me from unknown numbers and shit. Why did you stab her?"

"Why would I tell you for you to judge me more than you already are? Can you just give me some money and we go our separate ways?" Being around my mother wasn't going to lead to anything good. I'd rather get the fuck away from her and love that woman from a distance.

"Tell me why you stabbed her, and I'll think about giving it to you."

"Why must you play these stupid ass games?"

"Just answer my question, Chrissy. You always think I'm against you and shit. All I be trying to do is help you, but you're so fucking stubborn, you think everyone always got it out for your ass." She shook her head.

"I found out she was pregnant by Kon." Tears filled my eyes. Every time he crossed my mind, I wanted to hurt him just as much as he hurt me. I felt like stabbing Sapphire wasn't enough in my book. I know the shit sounded crazy, but he basically snatched my fucking life away from me.

For nine years, Kon was all I knew. He knew that hoe for five minutes and up and left my ass with basically nothing but a big ass empty ass house. After what I did, that house was going to be snatched from underneath me as well.

"And that was a good enough reason for you to stab the girl?"

"See, I knew you were going to fucking judge me." Rising from my seat, I went to storm off, but she caught me by the wrist.

"I'm not trying to judge you or anything. I just don't agree with the bullshit you did. It was a better way you could have handled the situation."

"Ma, I didn't come here for a fucking lecture. I came to see if you were going to help me or not."

"I swear sometimes I feel like all you see me as is a fucking ATM." Sucking her teeth, she went into her purse and pulled out her wallet. I glanced over taking a peek into her wallet to see what was in there. My mother wasn't broke, but she was far from rich as well. One thing was for sure, she had a whole lot of money in her wallet for someone that never liked to have cash on her. I started to ask why she was walking about with that much on her, but opted out of it, not wanting to piss her the fuck off.

She took five crisp hundred dollar bills and laid them down on the table in front of me. That wasn't even half of what she had in her wallet. I should have asked her for more, but I was lucky enough to get that much out of her.

"Thank you." I smiled and swiped the money off the table.

"Now, what?"

"I have to get me a ride out of here until shit cools down."

"So basically, you're running?"

"Whatever you want to call it."

"What about Stormie? You know she's going to hate you when she gets older for leaving her. If I were you, I'd go talk to Kon. He seems like that's all he wants."

"Did he say if she died?" That was really the only thing on my mind.

"He didn't say, but for your sake, you better hope like hell she didn't."

"I don't care if she did or didn't." I mumbled, rolling my eyes. If he knew I was the one who stabbed her, then she had to be alive, right? "I'll be right back. I have to go to the bathroom." Rising to my feet, I rushed to the bathroom to take a breather. I didn't have to use it, but I needed to get the hell away from her for a moment and get my thoughts together.

Pacing the bathroom floor, I sighed. I felt like I needed to get the hell away from there before Kon tried to kill me for stabbing Sapphire. I know I was in his life first, but that didn't mean he was going to choose me over her. My mother put thoughts in my mind and had me second guessing running away. If I was to, I'd be leaving behind Stormie and I didn't want her to resent me for the rest of her life.

I always told myself that I was never going to be anything like my mother. She never neglected me, but I thought I'd be far better off if she had.

"Stormie should understand, right?" I asked myself, steady pacing. "Who am I kidding? She's just a fucking child. I shouldn't let Kon run me away from my child. Fuck him and Sapphire."

I made up in my mind that I was going to face him head on. I was bold enough to stab her ass, I was going to be bold enough to let him know that I wasn't scared. Whatever he had planned for me, I could fucking handle it.

"Yeah, you got this shit," I told myself, gazing at my reflection in the mirror.

A toilet flushed and this woman stepped out of a stall, staring at me as if I had two fucking heads.

"The fuck are you looking at?" I mugged her through the mirror, and she left out of the bathroom without washing her hands. Nasty bitch.

Taking a deep breath, I exited the restroom prepared to suck it up and tell my mother she was right. As I neared her table, I noticed she was talking to this guy. The closer I got, I saw it was Kon and my heart stopped.

If he was there, she had to have ratted me out to him. And to think I was about to finally give her ass a fucking chance. The only reason she agreed to meet me here was to fucking hand me over to Kon not even knowing what he fucking had planned for me. The shit was fucked up.

Grabbing a menu off a nearby table, I hid my face with it and made a dash for the door. As soon as I got outside, I hopped into Thugga's car and got the hell out of there before anyone saw me.

I pulled over at the corner store down the street and went inside to purchase a sim card. My clammy hands trembled as I eased it into the phone and dialed my mother's number. It didn't take her long to pick up as if she had been waiting for me to call her or something.

"Chrissy?"

"How could you?"

"What are you talking about?"

"You told Kon you were meeting me there!"

"No, I didn't."

"Why are you lying? I saw him there with you."

"He was already there and came over to speak to me."

"That's a fucking lie!"

"How do you know? You weren't at the table with me."

"Kon's allergic to seafood!" That's the reason why I invited her there in the first place because I knew we wouldn't run into him. She called him there and didn't want to fucking admit the shit.

"Okay, so fucking what? I may have told him that I was meeting you, but that's what you want, right? To have him to yourself?"

"Kon wasn't coming to fucking talk to me, dummy! Kon wants my fucking head and you were prepared to help him get it! What type of mother are you?"

"I know damn well you of all people aren't judging my parenting skills when you want to fucking run away from your got damn problems because you fucked up. You was talking about leaving your got damn child behind and shit."

"At least I wasn't trying to hand her over to someone that will possibly fucking kill her!" Not wanting to hear anything else that bitch had to fucking say, I hung the phone up and pulled away from the curb.

Pulling back up to Thugga's house, I saw his car parked out front. "Shit."

I hurriedly pulled up behind his car and got out. Thanks to my mother, I was late getting back, and he'd know that I took his car without his permission.

Climbing out of the car, I went into the house, but didn't spot him. I slipped his keys onto the table by the front door and rubbed my hand up and down the nape of my neck. I treaded down the hallway toward Thugga's bedroom to see what he had new on my situation with Kon. He needed to get a move on the shit before he ended up killing my ass and my daughter be motherless.

I fixed my mouth to say something when I entered his doorway, but stopped when I saw him removing a police badge from his jeans and placing it into one of his drawers.

"You're a fucking cop!" I couldn't believe the shit I was seeing at the moment.

Thugga jumped and faced me. His eyes were as wide as saucers, and he knew he was caught red-handed.

"It's not what you think."

"How the fuck it's not when I just saw the fucking badge in your got damn hand?" My heart dropped to the pit of my stomach. "Oh, my God! You're a cop! Does that mean you're taking me to jail for stabbing Sapphire? I confessed to you. I'm so got damn stupid." Pacing the floor, I nibbled on my fingernails. The entire time, I was trying to stop myself from going to prison, and I'd been here with this nigga who could take me in the blink of an eye.

He neared me and I backed up away from him. I knew I shouldn't have brought my ass over here. Something told me to just go to Serenity's house, but I didn't know if I was going to be safe there.

"You don't have to be scared of me. If I wanted to do something to you or lock you up, don't you think I would have done it by now?"

He did kind of make sense.

"How did a cop get mixed up in some shit like this?"

Grabbing my hand, he pulled me over to the bed and I sat down on it.

"I've been plotting against Kon for years now. When he took my father out, he took everything from my family. That nigga was greedy as fuck and I vowed to pay his ass back at all costs. I joined the police force thinking it would have been easy to take his ass out, but I got tired of trying to do shit the legal way and got dirty just like him. I built my own empire from the ground up.

No one knows that I'm a cop but you. All I ask is that you keep my secret and I'll continue to help you."

"How come you aren't going to lock me up?"

"I promised that I was going to help you take his ass down and get your daughter back, and that's exactly what I'ma do."

"And you sure I don't have anything to worry about?" I

wanted to believe Thugga, but something deep down kept telling me that he wasn't to be trusted. I had to tread lightly around him just in case.

Sapphire

A couple days later...

Getting up from the bed, I slipped my feet into my slippers and made my way out of the bedroom to get breakfast started. Kon wasn't home which was a good thing because we were still on the outs about that argument the other day. He didn't even try to talk to me about the shit. I understood that he had a lot on his mind with trying to find Chrissy and everything, but that didn't give him the fucking right to put my feelings to the got damn side as if they didn't fucking matter.

Chrissy... I didn't really understand that bitch. I don't know how she could just disappear from her child's life as if it was nothing. I understood that she fucked up by stabbing me, and I was pretty sure she knew that, but she needed to suck shit up and suffer the consequences. I felt bad as fuck for Stormie to have her as a mother. I could only imagine what that poor child was going through.

Entering the kitchen, I went straight for the fridge, so I could hurry up and get breakfast started. I at least wanted to be halfway done by the time Stormie got up looking for something to eat.

As time went by, I slowly began not resenting her for what her mother did to me. But if I was ever to run across Chrissy on the fucking streets somewhere, I'd probably kill that fucking bitch. Killing someone really wasn't in me, but I couldn't just let her get away with the shit.

She fucked up my got damn life. She had me hating Kon because of her. The bitch took my child away from me. I even had nightmares the first couple of nights because of her. It's crazy as shit that I thought the motherfucker was going to come back and finish what she started. That was the reason why I hoped Kon found her, or I was going to the fucking cops and getting the bitch arrested.

"Sapphire?" Jumping, I turned to Stormie with my hand resting against my chest.

"I thought you were still sleeping."

She gazed up at me with her beady eyes. "Do you know when my mama is coming back?"

That was the sort of question she'd ask Kon and he'd come up with a fucking excuse whenever she did. At one point, she stopped asking and I thought she'd given up on the dumb bitch.

I stood there, nibbling on the corner of my lower lip, debating on what I was going to tell her. That was a question I couldn't really answer. I hoped the bitch wasn't coming back. I prayed Kon would put her ass six fucking feet under, but deep down, I kind of knew that shit wasn't going to fucking happen. If I went to the police and got the bitch locked up, she wouldn't be coming back.

"Sapphire?" Stormie brought me from my thoughts.

I knew I couldn't tell that child the truth, so I said, "I don't know, sweetie. That's something you'd have to ask your father. Are you hungry?" I quickly changed the subject before she got to asking me any more questions and I ended up with my fucking foot in my mouth.

"Do you have pancakes?"

That was one of her favorite things to eat in the morning time.

"You can't have breakfast without pancakes." I flaunted her

a smile and slid her plate down on the table in front of her.

She climbed into the chair, grabbing her fork. I poured her a glass of orange juice and placed the jug back into the fridge. Taking a deep breath, I squeezed my eyes shut. I just wished all this shit would be over.

"How about we go to the park when you're done eating?"

"Seriously?" Her eyes lit up.

"Of course. Go on and eat your food."

$$\infty\infty\infty$$

I pulled up to the park and Stormie jumped out of the car with her camera in her hand. She never liked to go to the park to play with the other children, she found it fascinating and would always take pictures of almost everything she saw. I told Kon a dozen of times that he had a little artist on his hands.

"Don't go too far!" I shouted behind her and made my way over to the nearest bench. I didn't really like outside that much with all of the bugs and all, but I did want to do something to take Stormie's mind off of her mother even if it was for a little while.

Getting comfortable on the bench, I pulled my phone out and dialed Sa'nai's number. I hadn't talked to her in the last couple of days and wanted to see what she was up to. Last I checked, she was still angry about us asking her to leave the Chrissy situation alone. Kon was more than capable of handling the shit on his own. But if I knew Sa'nai, she wasn't going to listen and still do whatever the fuck she wanted.

"Hello?"

"So, we going days without talking now?"

"You know the phone works both ways, right?" I could hear the sass in her voice.

"What were you up to?"

"Just leaving my doctor's appointment."

"How did it go?" I glanced out into the park to make sure I could still see Stormie. When my eyes landed on her, I went back to my conversation.

"It was good. My pressure was up a little bit."

"Why?"

"Too much going on. Enough about me though... where's Kon with the Chrissy problem? Every time I seem to ask Blessed about it, he just changes the conversation."

"'Cause that's something you don't need to be worrying about."

"They're taking too long to find the bitch if you asked me. Seems like to me, Kon doesn't really want to find her."

"And why do you say that?"

"If he really wanted to find her ass, he'd find her."

"It's not that simple, Sa'nai."

"The hell it ain't. Just think..." Sa'nai kept talking, but my mind drifted to Stormie and I immediately looked up in the direction I last saw her in. She wasn't there. I rose from the bench and neared the bush, not spotting her.

"Stormie!" I called out, feeling my heart thump rapidly in my chest. "Stormie!"

"Sapphire?" Sa'nai called my name. I completely forgot she was even on the phone.

"I have to call you back."

"What's going on, Sapphire? Is something wrong with Stormie?"

"She's not where I left her."

"The hell do you mean? She's not an object, Sapphire."

"She's not here!" I panicked. If I didn't find her and find her soon, Kon was going to fucking kill me.

"Where are you?"

"I brought her to the park to get out of the house. I told her not to go anywhere!"

"Calm down. Stop and breath." Squeezing my eyes shut, I took a few deep breaths. "Look around and see if you see her anywhere."

My eyes frantically searched the park from where I stood, but I still didn't see her. Maybe Chrissy had done a good thing by taking my child away from me. Clearly, I wasn't fit to take care of another human being if I lost this one.

"I still don't see her. What am I going to do?" Tears welled up in my eyes. All I could think about was what if something had happened to her. Kon would never forgive me...

"Call the police and text me which park you're at."

"You sure I should call the police?" I knew that Kon and Blessed were into some illegal ass shit and didn't know how he felt about using the police.

"Call them, then call Kon and let him know what's going on. I'm on my way."

She ended the call and right away, I was on the phone with the police. We weren't on there long before they notified me that they were sending someone out to the park. My heart dropped to the pit of my stomach as my thumb hovered over Kon's name.

For the longest, I had been pissed off at him about Chrissy and now the shoe was about to be on the other foot. He'd probably hate me for the rest of my life if I allowed something to happen to his daughter while she was in my care.

Sucking up my fears, I finally pressed his name and listened to the phone ring in my ear. With every chime of the phone, my heart pounded harder.

"Hello?" he finally answered, and I fell silent.

How was I supposed to tell the man I loved that I lost his fucking daughter? How was I supposed to say that she might never come back?

"Sapphire?"

"Kon?..." Tears streamed down my face.

"Yeah? Is everything alright?"

I swallowed the lump that formed in my throat.

"I lost Stormie!"

"What the fuck you mean, you lost her!"

My body trembled. I could only imagine his facial expression at the moment.

"I—I didn't mean to. I took her to the park and—"

"Where the fuck you at?" he cut me off. Out of the entire time we'd been talking, he'd never spoken to me in that manner before. I had a feeling that everything was about to fucking change.

"At David T. Kennedy Park." The line fell silent. I glanced down and saw that this nigga had hung the fucking phone up on me.

Five minutes later, I heard sirens in the distance. I didn't want to move from my spot, but I knew I had to meet the police and tell them what happened. Just as soon as I made it to the parking lot, they stepped out of the car.

"Were you the one that called the police?" the male cop asked as he shut the door and approached me.

"Yes." My hands were clammy and trembled.

"You mind telling us what happened?" the female officer questioned.

I wasted no time running down everything that happened

since the moment I realized Stormie was missing. By the time I was done telling them, Kon's car whipped into the parking lot almost on two wheels. My breath caught in my throat, not knowing what was going to happen once he made his way to me.

He hopped from the car and stormed directly up to me with a mug on his face. Without uttering a single word, his hand wrapped tightly around my throat and I could have sworn my feet dangled as he lifted me from the ground.

"Where the fuck is my daughter!" he barked, spit flying from his lips.

"I—I—"

Kon damn near cut off my circulation. My airways slowly began to close, and it was becoming impossible for me to breathe.

"Sir, you have to let go of her." The female officer eased toward us. Tears pooled at the brims of my eyes.

"If you don't release her, I will have no other choice but to arrest you," the male officer warned.

I didn't want to see Kon go to jail, but they were supposed to have arrested his ass the moment he placed his fucking hands on me.

He dropped me to the ground, and I sat there, caressing my neck. Kon's eyes locked with mine and they were dark and cold. I'd never seen his eyes like that before. But what did I expect? That was his child. She came before me and I respected that, but he didn't have to take his fucking anger out on me. Stormie was old enough to know not to fucking wonder off on her own. All of this wasn't my got damn fault, but I figured I was going to be the one who got blamed for it anyway.

"Why the fuck are you bitches still standing here! Get the fuck out there and find my got damn child!"

"Sir, you really need to calm down," the female officer tried to reason with him.

"I won't do shit 'til y'all find my got damn daughter."

"Ma'am, we have everything that we need. As soon as we know something, we'll be in contact." She extended her hand to me and helped me up off the ground. I nodded, hugging myself, watching them as they climbed into their car and pulled off.

I was so fucking embarrassed from how he treated me.

He glanced at me one more time and trekked into the park, so I rushed behind him.

"You don't have anything to say to me?" He ignored me and kept walking. "Kon!" I swiftly caught his arm, stopping him. He snatched away from me and mugged me.

"You had one fucking responsibility... watch my fucking child and you couldn't even do that."

Tears streamed down my face. "I was watching her. If you would have just told her the fucking truth about her mama, I wouldn't have had to bring her to the park to take her fucking mind off the shit!"

"So, you tryna say it's my fucking fault that Stormie's missing?"

"That's not what I'm saying."

"That's what the fuck it sounds like to me."

"Know what... I'm not 'bout to do this shit with you." I stormed away from him, heading for my car. I was over this fucking conversation and him as well.

As I pulled the door open to get into my car, Sa'nai pulled into the parking lot. I almost forgot that she said she was coming up there.

"Sapphire!" she shouted my name and I stopped. Jumping from her car, she jogged up to me and asked, "Did y'all find her?"

Tears streamed down my face. I didn't even want to face her after what happened.

"What happened?" I knew she was going to ask me that and I also knew she was going to get ready to kick Kon's ass once I told her what was wrong with me.

"He fucking blamed me for Stormie disappearing."

"Are you fucking serious?" She frowned and glanced around the park where we stood to see if she could spot him. "I'm going to kick his fucking ass. Where the hell he at?"

"I don't know. He went to look for her, but I looked for her everywhere. I told her not to go too far. Why she didn't listen to me?"

Sa'nai firmly wrapped her arms around me and I cried into her shoulder. "She's a child. They always do the complete opposite of what you tell them to do."

"What if something happened to her?"

"Wherever she is, I'm sure that she's fine. Come on and let's get out of here." She tugged on my arm, but I didn't budge.

"I don't want to go back to the house."

"You can come to mine. You know you're always welcomed there."

"Thanks."

I was going to go to Sa'nai's house for the moment to get my mind together, but then I was getting out there in the streets and doing whatever I possibly could to try and find Stormie. I wasn't going to be able to sleep or think clearly until I knew that she was all right.

Chrissy

"**M**ama, where are we going?"

I kept glancing in my rearview mirror to make sure no one was following me. I couldn't believe I had just pulled off basically snatching Stormie at the park from that bitch Sapphire. How dare Kon allow her to be around my child by herself. There was no fucking telling what she'd do to my child. People were crazy as fuck and would do anything for fucking attention.

"I'm taking you to my house," I told her.

"We going home?"

"Somewhat." I exhaled when I pulled onto Thugga's street.

I hadn't told him where I'd gone or what I was about to do. I had been watching Kon's house ever since I followed him home the day before. Ever since my mother put all those thoughts in my mind about leaving Stormie behind, I knew I had to come up with a way for me to get her. It wasn't the smartest move to make, but she was with her mother now, and knew that I hadn't deserted her.

Pulling into the driveway, I climbed out of the car and helped Stormie out of the back. Her eyes drifted up to the house and they lit up. Thugga's house wasn't anywhere near as huge as ours, but it was a decent size.

"Whose house is this?" she asked, and I wasn't sure how to answer the question.

"This is a friend's house."

"What kind of friend?"

"Just a friend. Come on."

Grabbing her hand, I led her up to the front door and into the house. Thugga was home, and I was terrified of what he was going to say once I brought her into the house. He'd welcomed me into his house, and I invited another guest in there without his permission.

"Who's this?" His voice caught me off guard and goosebumps coursed down my spine.

Taking a deep breath, a smile passed my lips and I turned, facing him. "Thugga, this is my daughter Stormie."

"Who is this mama?" Stormie's eyes met mine.

"This is the friend I was telling you about."

Her gaze met Thugga's. "Who are you? Why are we here?"

He kneeled down to eye level with her and said, "I've been helping your mama try to get you back."

"Get me back?" Her brow rose as she stared at me.

"Yeah. She's been staying with me for a while."

"When are we going home? I don't want to be here."

Kneeling, I gripped her by the shoulders and stared deep into her eyes. "Why would you say something like that." Stormie has always been sweet. Maybe she had been around Sapphire a little too long, and that was my fault. I shouldn't have ever left her over there like that in the first place.

"But I don't like him."

"Stormie!" My blood boiled at the shit that was coming out of her mouth.

"It's okay. She doesn't know me, so she has the right not to like me," Thugga spoke up. I taught her better than that.

"No, it's not. This shit isn't acceptable." Roughly gripping her by the forearm, I dragged her down the hallway to one of Thugga's guest bedrooms. Shoving her into the room, I shut the door behind us. "What the hell is wrong with you?"

"I wanna go home." She stomped her foot, pouting, folding her arms across her chest.

"You're not going anywhere. I went through a lot of trouble to get you here with me and you're going to stay whether you like it or not."

"Take me back to Sapphire!"

"Sapphire don't give a damn about your ass."

"Yes, she do. She bought me this camera." She flashed this expensive camera in front of my face, and I slapped it down. It crashed to the floor and broke into pieces.

Tears shimmered in her eyes. I didn't feel bad about breaking that stupid ass camera because Sapphire was the one who bought it. I didn't need her doing stuff for my child that I could do myself.

She kneeled, picking the pieces up in her tiny hands. "You broke it." Her watery gaze met mine.

"You shouldn't have been gloating about it."

"Take me back to Sapphire!" Dropping the camera, she straightened her posture.

"I'm not taking you anywhere. You better go watch T.V. or something."

I went to leave out of the room, but she shouted, "Take me back or I'ma call and tell her to come get me." Her arms folded across her chest as she mugged me.

"How you gon' call her without a phone?"

She was silent for a moment, then said, "I'll just walk."

"Your little ass ain't walking anywhere."

"Fine. I'll just tell your friend to take me."

She stormed passed me and I gripped her by the forearm, yanking her back. "You mean to tell me that you like her better than me?"

"You're being mean! You left me with them and never came back. Sapphire would never do something like that!"

My hand connected with the side of her face. It just did something to me to hear her fucking compare me to that bitch. She was my child. I fucking birthed her, and she chose the got damn enemy over me.

Tears filled my eyes. I slapped the shit out of her again and she dropped to the floor. "I'm your fucking mama, not her!" Yanking my belt off, I took it straight across her thighs and she screamed out in pain. "You hear me! Me!" I hit her again and she balled up into the fetal position. I beat Stormie over and over with that belt, watching the lesions and welts form on her skin.

The idea that Sapphire had tried to replace me in my child's life pissed me the fuck off. This was the exact thing I was afraid of, but I was so busy trying to get rid of that bitch and get Kon back, I didn't have time for Stormie. Now she was treating me like I didn't mean shit and didn't have any fucking feelings. My hand lifted to hit her again and was caught in mid swing.

"What the hell are you doing!" Thugga barked, yanking the belt away from me.

I gazed down at Stormie as she lay balled up whimpering. I hadn't realized just how far I had taken things until Thugga snatched the belt away from me.

"I'm-I'm sorry."

Stormie picked herself up off the floor and ran out of the room. I tried to go behind her, but Thugga stopped me.

"What the hell were you thinking?"

"I wasn't." My eyes lowered. I was embarrassed as fuck at

my intentions. I'd never laid a hand on her before. My mind was all sorts of fucked up, and I blamed it all on Sapphire and Kon.

"You know that's fucking child abuse, right? I could take you to jail for that shit."

I snatched away from him. "You'd take me to jail for beating Stormie, but not for stabbing Sapphire. That shit makes no sense."

"You fucking wanna go to jail for stabbing her?"

"No."

"Alright then."

I brushed my hair back out of my face with my hands.

"I'm going to check on my daughter."

"You put yo' hands on her again, I'ma beat your fucking ass," he warned and left out of the bedroom.

Taking a deep breath, I left out of the room behind him in search of Stormie. I heard sobs coming from the bathroom door.

Knock! Knock!

The weeping stopped. "Stormie?" I nibbled on the corner of my lower lip. "I know that you're mad at me, but can you come out, so I can talk to you."

"Go away!" she shouted and sniffled.

"Stormie, if you don't bring your ass out of that bathroom right fucking no—" Thugga strolled past me and eyed me. I was trying not to lose my cool, but she was pissing me the fuck off. I jiggled the doorknob and she had it locked. "Stormie, please come out."

"Leave me alone."

"I promise that I won't hurt you again."

She fell silent on the other side of the door. My heart was broken because I felt like she was terrified of me.

"Stormie, you know I love you with all of my heart."

"Just give her time, Chrissy." I shot Thugga daggers. He was all in my fucking business. This had nothing to do with him.

"No one was fucking talking to you."

He frowned and continued into the living room.

Placing my hand flat on the door, I said, "I'm really sorry, Stormie."

She snatched the door open and mugged me. "I fucking hate you!" She bumped me, running out of the room and one of the doors slammed, causing me to jump.

I really was sorry for how I treated her. I just hoped she knew that.

Kon

My finger grazed my piece and jaw muscles tensed up. I was fed the fuck up with all of this bullshit. My blood boiled and all I wanted to do was paint the entire city fucking red. My patience was running thin with that bitch Stephanie. It was like she was purposely running me around in a got damn circle.

Ever since Stormie went missing, I felt like that was Thugga trying to get one over on me. She was only gone a day and I was going fucking crazy. There was no telling what he was doing to her, and I damn sure didn't want to think about something being wrong with her.

I still couldn't fucking believe Sapphire was so got damn careless to lose my fucking child. I guess it wasn't good enough that she lost my fucking seed.

"I just need more time," she pleaded with tears in her eyes. In my fucking opinion, I gave her too much fucking time in the world.

I scratched the side of my head with my strap. "Yo' time is—" My words got cut short at the ring of my phone. Pulling it out of my pocket, I glanced down at the screen. An unknown number was calling me.

Normally, I didn't answer unknown numbers, but I got this gut feeling that I couldn't let this one slip by me. Lifting my index finger at a sobbing Stephanie, I answered the phone without speaking.

"Daddy?" I heard Stormie's voice with a sniffle.

I took the phone away from my ear and gazed at it in awe, thinking I was tripping. "Stormie?"

Stephanie's eyes bucked as I rose from the couch. "Can you come get me?"

"Where are you? Are you hurt?"

"I'm with mama. She beat me."

My hand balled into a fist. "That's who took you?"

Not once did the idea of Chrissy taking her crossed my mind. She had dropped her off with me and never looked back. I'd gotten to the point of thinking that she wanted nothing to do with her anymore.

"She beat you?" So many thoughts of me beating Chrissy's ass coursed through my mind.

"Yes." She wept, and that shit crushed my fucking heart. "She broke the camera Sapphire bought me too."

"Do you know where you are?"

"No. At a house with a friend of hers."

"What friend? Serenity?"

"No. It's a man."

"Do you remember his name?"

"It's—" She paused for a moment. "I have to go."

"Are you gon' tell me who the friend is or how I can—" Before I could finish my sentence, the phone disconnected. "Fuck!" I bellowed.

"That was your daughter... we should be good, right?"

"I don't know what makes you think that." Lifting my hand, I aimed my gun at her.

"Kon, please," she begged.

"This shit yo' fucking fault." If I didn't have to run behind her and shit, I would have been in place where Chrissy couldn't take my daughter. If her dumb ass was on her toes, none of this shit would have happened and Thugga would have been out of the got damn picture.

"Kon, you really don't wanna do—"

Pow!

The bullet crashes through her forehead and her body slumped to the floor. That was some shit I should have done a long time ago. I was becoming soft as fuck and that's how come everyone kept one up on me.

Tucking my gun in my waistline, I slipped my phone from my pocket. I quickly dialed the clean-up crew number.

"I need the living room cleaned in the apartment. Don't take all fucking day." I ended the call before they could even respond.

Strolling to the front door, I dialed my contact that I had at the police station. I been learned early that if you wanted to be successful in the streets, then you needed to have a few important people in your back pocket.

"Yeah, Kon?" Samantha answered the phone.

"I need you to get me a location on a phone number."

"What's the number?"

I rattled the number off to her and listened to her type away on the computer. When Stormie first went missing, she was the first person I called. She told me there really wasn't anything she could do about it, but she'd keep an eye out.

"You have something to write the address down with?"

"Just tell it to me; I'll remember it."

She quickly told me the address and I ended the call. I didn't want to say anything else to her and end up forgetting.

When I jumped into my car, I swiftly typed the address in my GPS. I couldn't wait to lay eyes on Stormie and make sure that she was okay. I couldn't wait to get my fucking hands on Chrissy. She didn't want to come around me because she already knew I was at her ass for stabbing Sapphire. The bitch could have handled the situation better than she had though. Had me out here thinking that Thugga or someone else had taken her.

I pulled onto the street and stopped a couple houses down just to scope the place out and see who all was there. I didn't see a car in the driveway and prayed they hadn't left. If Chrissy's crazy ass had put her hands on Stormie, there was no telling what else she would have done as well.

After sitting there for a good ten minutes and not noticing anything, I climbed out of the car and went up to the front door. I stood there with my hands in my pockets after knocking on the door. No one came to it. I had already Made up in my mind that I wasn't leaving there without my child. If I had to sit here all fucking day, I would. Chrissy was about to give me some motherfucking answers.

Stepping off of the porch, I went around back, so I could find somewhere to gain entry. Picking up a rock by the back door, I bashed the window in on the door and slipped my arm through it, unlocking the door. Entering the house, I eased my piece from my waistline and looked around.

Even though there weren't any cars outside, that didn't mean I was in the house alone. I'd rather be safe than sorry.

I crept down the hallway and stopped when I heard a television playing. Pressing my ear against the door, I stood there to see if I could hear anything else. For a while, all I heard was the television, then Stormie giggled. My heart pumped rapidly in my chest as I slowly turned the door-knob.

I stared at the back of her head as she sat at the foot of the bed. Tears glistened in my eyes. I somewhat thought that when she went missing, I was never going to see her again. With the line of work that I was in, people went missing all the time and were never found.

"Stormie?" I called out her name and she jumped from the bed.

Her eyes lit up when they say me and she ran over, wrapping her arms around my waist. "I knew you were going to find me."

"Are you okay?" I pushed her back away from me by the shoulders and examined her face.

"Yes." Her eyes lowered as if she had done something wrong.

"Where did she hurt you at?" She took a step back away from me and that's when I noticed the bruises all over her legs and thighs. Chrissy lost her fucking mind, putting her got damn hands on her like that. She'd never whooped Stormie a day in her fucking life. She was taking her anger for me out on our daughter and the shit made me want to beat the brakes off her fucking ass. "Where is she?"

"She said she was going to the store."

"And she left you here by yourself?"

"She told me that I couldn't go with her." Tears cascaded down her cheeks. "Please take me home. I don't want to be here anymore."

"I'm taking you home; you don't have to worry about all that."

I dialed Blessed's number and listened as the phone rang in my ear. Once he had learned of Stormie's disappearance, he had been going non-stop just as I had. She was like a daughter to him as well, and he wanted to make the mother-fucker who took her pay.

"Yeah?" he answered.

"I need you to come pick Stormie up."

"You found her?" I could hear the excitement in his voice.

"Yeah. I'm 'bout to text you the address now."

Disconnecting the call, I texted him the address and slipped the phone back into my pocket. "Let's get you out of here." Picking Stormie up into my arms, I carried her toward the front door. I noted the few pictures I saw around the house. They were of a guy and what I assumed was his family. I hadn't ever seen him before, but he damn sure was going to fucking pay for helping Chrissy's dumb ass kidnap my fuck-ing seed.

I took Stormie out to the car and we sat there until Blessed arrived. When he got there, he jumped out of the car and rushed up to mine, pulling her out. I watched the tears stream down his cheeks as he squeezed her.

"I—I can't breathe," she barely managed to get out.

"Sorry." He chuckled. "I just missed you, that's all."

I climbed out of the car and gazed at him over the hood.

"Who had her?"

"Chrissy's dumb ass." Normally, I didn't talk foul about Chrissy in front of Stormie, but I was pissed the fuck off.

"So, what you gon' do 'bout it?"

I hadn't really thought about all that. I just knew that something was going to have to be done. If I didn't do anything, she wasn't going to stop. She'd just continue trying to go after Sapphire because I no longer wanted her, and she'd continue to do dumb shit when it came to Stormie. She might actually put her in more harm's way.

Never had I ever thought that Chrissy would cause harm to her own child, but she was desperate. A scorned woman was capable of anything and I was going to protect my child at all costs, even if it was from her own mother.

"I'll figure it out. Just get her out of here."

Nodding, he headed back to his car. I shut my door and treaded back to the house. I wasn't leaving that mother-fucker until Chrissy returned. I didn't give a damn if it was days later; I was going to sit my ass right there in that living room and patiently wait for her ass.

Five hours later, I saw lights flash against the house and knew that someone had returned. I wasn't sure if it was Chrissy or that so-called friend she was staying with. Which-ever one it was, they were in for a rude awakening when they walked through that front door.

It pissed me the fuck off that she took that long to go to the got damn store. If I hadn't come when I did, Stormie would have still been in that house alone. I don't know what was wrong with that crazy motherfucker. She was nowhere near old enough to be home alone. That alone said she wasn't fit to be a got damn parent.

The locked turned and I grabbed my piece off the coffee table, gently resting it in my lap. Chrissy stepped through the door with shopping bags in her hands. She was so wrapped up in herself that she hadn't even noticed I was sitting there.

"This the type of shit we on now?" At the sound of my voice, she jumped and dropped the bags to the floor. Her eyes expanded when they landed on me. I rose from the couch, tightly clutching my gun.

"K-Kon, what are you doing here?"

I slowly neared her. Thoughts of her putting her got damn hands on Stormie seeped into my mind. I pictured myself choking the got damn life out of her ass.

"You weren't expecting to see me, huh?" A smirk crept up onto my face. "You thought that you were just going to kidnap my fucking seed and get away with the shit?"

"She's my daughter!"

I chuckled, scrubbing my hand across my mouth. "Oh, she's your fucking daughter now?" That shit was fucking hilarious to me. "Was she your fucking daughter when you dropped her off at the house with me and never came back? Was she your fucking daughter when you were more worried 'bout who the fuck I was fucking and letting someone else raise her?"

"I was coming back for her. That's why I took her in the first place. I knew you weren't ever going to let me see her again."

Boom!

I punched the wall directly next to her head and she jumped.

"Damn right I wasn't. You thought you were just going to fucking take my fucking child away from me and get away with the shit. Sapphire didn't fucking deserve the shit you did to her."

"Fuck Sapphire!"

Boom!

My fist hit the wall again. "You're testing my fucking patience right now."

Her eyes squeezed shut and tears cascaded down her

cheeks. She opened her eyes and stared me straight in the face. "Why her, Kon?"

"Does it really fucking matter?"

"Yes, it matters. You let her come in and ruin what we had together. Wasn't I always good to you? I loved you and you kicked me to the curb for some bitch you barely even know."

"That's your got damn problem now. You're so fucking worried 'bout what the fuck I got going on and not worried 'bout what you're supposed to be worried 'bout. Stormie should have been your main fucking concern, instead you fucking beat her!" I shoved my gun underneath her chin. "I think you really wanted to piss me the fuck off·

"Kon, please." Her lower lip trembled as she gazed at me.

"Did you show Stormie any fucking mercy when you took your got damn anger out on her?" Dropping my hand, I scrubbed the free one across my mouth again. "Fuck!"

Why the fuck did she make me have to do this shit? All she had to do was leave shit alone and go on with her fucking life, but no... she couldn't do it. She had to take shit beyond repair, and now I was going to have to put her out of her fucking misery.

I didn't want to end Chrissy's life, but I had to do whatever necessary to ensure that she couldn't cause harm to anyone else I loved.

"Kon, we can talk about this."

"There isn't shit to talk 'bout!"

Lifting my hand, I sent a bullet crashing through her skull. Blood and brain matter splattered all over the wall. I stood there, gazing at Chrissy as she lay against the wall with her eyes opened.

"Fuck!" I bellowed and got the fuck out of there. I should have stuck around and handled the motherfucker that helped her kidnap my fucking child, but Stormie needed me. I had to go make sure she was all right and let her know that she'd never see her mother again. I was sure she'd be angry with me for taking her away from her, but one day, she'd understand why I did it.

Climbing back into my car, I sped all the way to Blesssed's house to pick her up. When I got there, she was sleeping peacefully in her bedroom. He made sure to keep her a room there for whenever she stayed the night with him. It wasn't often, but I knew he was going to end up having her more since her mother was no longer in the picture.

"What did you do?" Blessed appeared at my side and questioned me. I kept my eyes trained on Stormie as she slept.

"What I had to."

"You think she'll ever forgive you for that?"

"I don't know, but I hope so."

"Don't tell her. She may have been pissed the fuck off with her now, but that was still her mother. Tell her she left or something. I know you don't want to spend the rest of your life with her hating you."

I've never lied to Stormie before and damn sure didn't want to start now, but Blessed was right. I knew she'd never forgive me for something like that.

"Daddy?" She softly called out, gaining my attention. Taking one final look at Blessed, I neared the bed, taking a seat on the edge.

"Yeah, sweetheart?"

"Where's mama?"

I glanced over my shoulder at Blessed. He nodded and

disappeared away from the door.

"After you left, I stayed and had a talk with your mother. She told me that she wanted to leave, but I told her she wasn't going anywhere with you." Tears glistened in her eyes. I hated how easy that lie rolled off of my tongue to her.

"She left me?"

"I know it may hurt right now, but it's probably for the best. I promise you that you don't have to ever worry 'bout me leaving you."

"Where's Sapphire?"

I don't know how come I didn't know that she was going to ask about her. I had placed Sapphire to the back of my mind after she came up missing and our little altercation. I blamed her for everything when I knew that wasn't the fucking case. The way I treated her, there was no coming back from that shit.

"Probably at home."

"Did you tell her that my camera broke?"

"Sapphire and I aren't really talking right now."

"How come?"

"She lost you."

"She didn't lose me. I left with mama, remember?"

"That was before I knew that."

"Is she coming back?"

"I don't know."

"She has to." Her eyes got watery. It was at that moment that I realized that Stormie loved Sapphire just about as much as I did.

"We'll discuss this later. For now, I have to get you home." I picked her up from the bed, let Blessed know I was leaving, and left.

Sa'nai

It had been a week since they found Chrissy's body and I wasn't going to lie and say I wasn't surprised because I damn sure was. I didn't think Kon had it in him to actually kill his baby's mother, but the son of a bitch did. When Blessed told me that, I was shocked as shit. I really thought I was going to have to go out there and kill the bitch my damn self. People thought I was joking when I said I was going to handle her ass if he hadn't. I was serious as a fucking heart attack. That bitch caused harm to my best friend. No way I was about to stand around and let that shit happen again on my watch.

Everything was slowly getting back to normal. I had my first doctor's appointment and the shit still seemed surreal that I was pregnant. Of course, Blessed had come with me and we both couldn't wait to find out what we were having, but that was a while from now.

"Where you going now?" he questioned me as we left out of the office.

I stopped at my car and hit the fob. "I was thinking about grabbing some lunch." I didn't have to go back to work since my appointment was in the middle of the day. I was hungry as hell and felt like I could eat an entire fucking horse at this point.

"I would join you, but I gotta go meet up with Kon."

"Again? About what this time?"

Blessed was pissing me the fuck off. Every time I turned around he was going out somewhere to meet up with Kon's ass. I thought that since they handled Chrissy, I'd have more time with him, but I guess I was wrong.

"You know I got shit to handle. Don't act brand new to the shit now, Nai."

"Don't you think I wanna spend time with you!"

"Here you go with this shit again. I'm 'bout to bounce before you blow everything out of fucking proportion." He backed away from me.

"Are you fucking serious right now?" I sighed, shifting all of my weight to my right side.

"Love you," was all he said before turning and sauntering to his car.

"Ugh!" I climbed into mine and slammed the door behind me.

Pulling out my phone, I texted Sapphire to see where she was at and if she wanted to grab lunch with me. Ever since her breakup with Kon, she had been burying herself in her work. I didn't think the shit was healthy, but it was her way to cope with what happened. If you asked me, Kon was a bitch for the way he handled shit. I still couldn't believe he tried to blame her for Stormie's disappearance. Then the motherfucker didn't even have the decency to let her know that he found her. I had to tell her because she'd been sad as fuck and blaming herself as well. I hated seeing her like that. Once she got back to work, I didn't even bother nagging her so much about her work ethic because I knew she needed something to take her mind off shit.

Sapphire: *I'm at work and probably will be for a while.*

Me: *Okay, I'll just bring lunch to you. You have to eat, right?*

Sapphire: *I guess.*

Just from the message alone, I could tell she wasn't feeling me popping up on her ass, but I didn't give a damn. I didn't want to spend lunch alone, so she was going to have to deal with me for the time being. Plus, I wanted to make sure she was truly all right. Sapphire could tell me anything, but I knew deep down, she was hurting like a motherfucker behind her breakup. I hated seeing her like that. If I could take away her pain, I would. I wouldn't even dare tell her to go running back to Kon after she told me how he treated her in that fucking park. It was her who stopped me from shoving my got damn foot up his fucking ass.

It was niggas like Kon that pissed me the fuck off. He thought that he did no wrong or made no fucking mistakes. I got that he was angry that Stormie went missing and he didn't know where the hell she was, but he had to take Sapphire's feelings into consideration as well. She felt like shit for that happening on her watch. She was already beating her damn self up about it. He should have tried to handle her more gently than he did. But it really didn't matter anymore. I was going to try my best to uplift her and take her mind off that jackass.

Pulling out of the parking lot, I headed to *Jackie's* this soul food restaurant to grab us something to eat. It was what I was craving now, and I wanted some red velvet cake. I was sure Sapphire didn't mind. More than likely, she was going to be too fucking busy to touch her food in the first place.

After grabbing our lunch, I headed straight to her office. It was hard as fuck trying to carry all that food and our drinks into the building, but I managed without spilling too much.

"I should have gotten a cup holder," I mumbled underneath my breath, watching the fruit punch roll down the front of my white shirt. That shit was going to be hard as fuck to get out.

Stepping off of the elevator, I flashed Sasha a smile and sauntered toward Sapphire's door.

"Is she expecting you?"

"Yup." I tossed over my shoulder and struggled to open the door. Sasha rushed over and grabbed it for me. "Thank you."

"You're welcome." She smiled and shut the door behind me.

Sapphire was sitting at her messy ass desk on the phone with strands of hair falling over into her face. Her ponytail looked as if she had done the shit in the fucking dark. Blowing her strands of hair back out of her face, she continued her conversation on the phone.

"Yes, I have an opening for that day." She picked at her fingernails, but didn't even bother to look at her calendar to be sure.

I scrunched my face up at her messy ass office. This shit was nothing like Sapphire and I really wished she'd get back on her shit.

Her feelings for Kon must have really ran deep because I had never seen her act like that before behind a breakup. Sure, it wasn't anything new for her to toss herself into her work, but it damn sure didn't happen like this.

"Sapphire?" I whispered and she gave me her index finger. I wanted her to get the fuck off the phone and give me her undivided attention. If I didn't do something, she was going to fucking lose herself more than she already had.

"Yes, I'll put you on the schedule and have Sasha get back to you." She ended the call and went to dial another number, but I snatched the phone away from her.

"Have you seen yourself?"

"I've been trying to avoid the mirrors."

"That explains the hair." I mumbled underneath my breath.

"What?" Her eyes quickly snapped in my direction from her personal phone. If I didn't know any better, I would have thought that she was trying to use the motherfucker to call whoever she intended on calling from her work phone.

"You look a fucking mess. This office looks got damn horrible. You really need to get up and do something about this shit."

"I will straighten everything out."

"When?"

"I'm going to handle it!" She shouted and her eyes squeezed shut.

I tossed my hands up in the air. "I just tryna help you out. You don't have to take yo' fucking anger out on me.

"I'm sorry Nai. I just feel like I'm losing my got damn mind."

"When's the last time you ate?"

"I don't know."

"Here, you need to eat something." I dropped the bag down on the desk. "Put something on your stomach."

Sighing, she grabbed the bag and pulled the food from it. "Have you heard anything from Kon?"

That should have been the last thing on her mind, but it seemed that wasn't the case.

"Just the same shit that I told you yesterday."

"I'm just glad that Stormie's back home where she belonged. I was really worried about her."

"I know."

She took a bite of her fried chicken and I noted the expression of relief that she made. That probably was the first thing she had eaten all day. She really needed to take better care of herself.

"I still can't believe what happened to Chrissy."

I sat her work phone down on the desk in front of me and took a seat in one of the chairs.

"Now that she's gone, you need to move on with your life. You don't have to worry about her trying to cause harm to you again."

"I know, but I just can't get her off my mind."

"Her or him?"

"I don't even want to talk about him." Her eyes lowered and she dropped her fork onto her plate and slumped back into her chair.

"You need to let that shit out, Sapphire. If you don't, shit just going to get worse. I hate seeing you like this."

"I'm good on Kon. Maybe it just wasn't meant to be."

"Are you sure about that?"

"Let's talk about something else before I put your ass out." She brushed her hair back with her hands and picked her fork back up.

"I went to the doctor today."

I may have changed the subject, but I was still worried about her. Hopefully, shit would get better.

Sapphire

I briefly took my eyes away from my computer and noticed that it was going on eleven. I told Sasha that I was going to stay a while. I didn't know that much time had slipped away from me.

My mind had been in complete overdrive since my breakup. It was the only way I was going to be able to handle shit. Sa'nai wasn't feeling my work ethic now, but it was the only thing keeping me sane.

Shutting my laptop, I gathered my things and rose from my chair. I was beyond exhausted and hungry again. I damn sure didn't feel like going home and cooking, so I'd just have to stop somewhere to grab something to eat along the way home.

Lately I hadn't felt like doing much but working. Almost every night, I was eating fast food and that shit definitely wasn't like me.

Climbing into the car, I stopped by *Crab City* to grab me something to eat and went straight home. My tub and a bottle of wine was calling me. I pulled into my driveway and grabbed my things from the car. When I got into the house, I kicked my shoes off at the door and went straight to my bedroom. Placing my food on the dresser, I unbuttoned my shirt. I froze in place when I realized Kon was sitting on the edge of my bed.

"What the fuck, Kon!" My heart thumped rapidly in my chest. He scared the shit out of me.

"Where you been?"

"Work," was all I said, making my way into the bathroom to start my bubble bath.

"You were at work this late? You haven't worked this late in a while."

"Yeah, because I was too busy tryna stay alive from your crazy ex." Or did he forget that shit? Spinning around, I faced him as he leaned against the doorframe. "What are you doing in my shit?" He was the last person I wanted to see.

"I came to talk to you."

"We don't have shit to talk about."

He turned the water off and I folded my arms over my chest.

"I know that you're angry with me." He gripped me by the hand and pulled me into the bedroom. He pushed me down onto the bed by the shoulders.

"I really don't feel like this shit, Kon."

Kneeling down in front of me, he locked eyes with me and said, "I know I probably hurt you, but you have to understand that I was pissed the fuck off about Stormie being missing. I didn't know what the fuck to do at the time and I took shit out on you."

"You don't have to apologize."

"Yes, I do. It was wrong as fuck and I'm sorry."

Tears glistened in my eyes as I stared back at him. "It's okay."

"You sure?"

"Yeah, long as she was found safely, that's all that really matters."

"She's been asking about you ever since she got back home."

"Really?" My eyes lit up. I had grown fond of Stormie. She was practically like a daughter to me. I know she was probably going through a complicated time at the moment with her mother being dead and all. I couldn't possibly understand what she was going through.

"Yeah, I was wondering if you wanted to come back home with me."

Those were the words I had been waiting to hear for the longest. Now that he had said them, I wasn't sure if that was the best idea.

"I don't know about that." Swiftly, I sprouted from the bed, giving him my back and hugged myself.

"Why not?" I felt his presence behind me. As much as I wanted to just forgive him and go running back to him, I knew it probably wasn't a good idea.

Our entire relationship was built rather quickly, and I should have known that soon it would come tumbling down. I hurt a woman in the process of trying to get what I wanted. I hurt her so bad emotionally that she hurt me physically. Maybe that was karma coming back to whoop my ass.

"Maybe it was meant for us to break up."

His hands landed on my shoulders and goosebumps coursed all over my skin.

"You know I love you. Me and Stormie both."

I spun around on my heels, facing him. "You put your hands on me, Kon. You made me feel like a fool and embarrassed me."

"I know and I'm sorry. I promise to never put my hands on you again."

I nibbled on the corner of my lower lip, debating on what I really wanted to do.

Taking a step closer to him, I said, "If you do, I promise you'll fucking regret it."

"Pack your stuff."

He rushed into my closet and grabbed my suitcases.

"What about my food?"

"You can eat that shit in the car. Hurry up, so I can pick Stormie up."

"Where is she anyway?"

"Over there with Blessed and Sa'nai."

"I wonder how come she didn't tell me she was over there."

"Probably 'cause she didn't want to worry you." He began stuffing clothes into the suitcase. He wasn't even putting outfits together. I knew if I didn't want to end up going to work tacky as fuck, I needed to intervene.

"I think I can pack my own clothes."

"Okay." He pecked me gently on the lips. "I'll be up front whenever you're ready." He left out of the room, leaving me to gather my clothes.

When I was done, I grabbed my two suitcases and rolled them into the living room. Kon was comfortable on the couch with a blunt between his lips.

"I'm ready," I made known.

"Okay." Putting the blunt out, he rose to his feet and grabbed my bags. I made sure to return to the room for my food; I wasn't leaving there without it and I was starving.

We made it to Blessed's house. I thought about going inside to speak to them, but I was tired as hell and opted out of it. I just wanted to make it back to the house, so I could shower and climb in bed.

Kon got out of the car and went into the house to get Stormie. With how late it was, I figured she would have been sleep, but she wasn't. She was all smiles when they emerged from the house. I was excited to see that she was doing well despite the passing of her mother. Kon told me that he hadn't told her he was the reason she was dead. I completely understood why he didn't want to—he could possibly lose his daughter forever.

When she climbed into the car, she wrapped her arms around my neck from behind. "Sapphire! I missed you."

"I missed you too." I pecked her on the cheek.

"Sit back in yo' seat," Kon instructed her, and she slipped back, fastening her seatbelt.

"Did daddy tell you about my camera?" I could hear the disappointment in her voice. My eyes cut to him and he shook his head.

"What happened?" I questioned him.

"Chrissy broke it."

My hands balled into fists. I knew she only did that shit because somehow, she found out I was the one who bought it. I didn't understand how she could have so much fucking rage toward me that she'd hurt her own daughter in such a manner.

On the ride over, he told me all about Chrissy beating her. I was disgusted by the news. Stormie was such a sweet child. She rarely got in trouble whenever she was around me. To hear that Chrissy took her fucking anger out on that innocent child made me want to bring the bitch back to life just to kill her all over again.

"It's okay. I'll get you another one and it's going to be better than the last." I glanced back at her and she sported a smile. I bought that camera for her because I believed in her. She was great with that shit and I knew she could grow up to do amazing things.

"Thank you."

I relaxed in my seat for the rest of the ride to the house. When we arrived, Kon grabbed a sleeping Stormie from the back seat and carried her into the house. As he took her into her bedroom, I went into ours and started the shower. I wanted a bubble bath, but it had gotten late, and I wasn't up for it anymore.

Stripping out of my clothes, I stepped over into the shower. I wasn't in there long before I felt Kon pressing up against me from behind. Goosebumps washed over my entire body. I desperately missed being in his presence. I missed his touch. The feel of his lips caressing my skin.

"Mmhmm." A light moan escaped my lips as his glided against the nape of my neck.

My pussy purred. It seemed like forever since I last had sex. My body was yearning for a climax, and I damn sure was about to get me one.

Gripping me by the shoulder, he spun me around where I faced him. His fingertips glided against my shoulders and I sank my teeth into my lower lip.

"I missed you." His eyes embraced my frame. I loved the way he always looked at me.

"I missed you too." Our lips meshed and my body crashed into his. Gripping me by the shoulders again, he roughly turned me around where my back faced him. His hand glided up to my neck and he pushed me over, putting an arch in my back.

His fingers glided against my pussy and he sucked the juices off of them.

"Fuck me," I moaned. My pussy thumped to feel him.

He positioned his dick at my opening. I grabbed it and eased him inside me. My eyes rolled to the back of my head. His dick rapidly hit my spot and my legs trembled.

"Fuck!" I moaned out.

Kon wrapped my hair tightly around his hand and jerked my head back. I felt my juices running down my inner thighs mixing in with the water.

I threw my ass back on his dick, matching his rhythm.

"I missed the shit out this pussy."

I felt my climax forming. He lifted my right leg, holding it in the crease of his arm. His dick went deeper damn near touching my chest.

"Fuck!"

I gently massaged my clit. My entire body shivered, and I finally erupted.

"That's what the fuck I'm talking about."

He gave me a few more pumps and released his seeds inside of me. Dropping my leg, he pecked me on the lips. We cleaned each other up and got dressed. Since I was going to bed, I slipped on one of his t-shirts and a pair of panties.

"Where you going?" he questioned me as I made me way toward the bedroom door.

"I'm going to check on Stormie."

"She's sleep."

"I know. I just wanna see her."

After her being away from me for so long, I just wanted to look at her for a while. After all, she was the closest thing I had to a child. Stormie and I had this connection that I could barely explain.

Stopping at her bedroom door, I eased it open and stared at her from the doorway. She was so cute, sleeping peacefully in her bed. I couldn't understand how something so sweet could come from something so got damn evil.

"Sapphire?" She called out my name. I hadn't even noticed she was awake.

"Yeah?" I eased further into her bedroom and took a seat on the edge of the bed.

"I'm really glad that you're back."

I softly stroked her hair back out her face. "Me too, sweetheart."

"Can you sleep with me tonight?" I was shocked hearing her ask me that.

"Sure." Pulling the covers back, I climbed over into the bed with her. My head hit the pillow and she snuggled underneath me. It didn't take long before I was out for the count.

Blessed

I took a toke from the blunt and blew the smoke out. My eyes scanned the street. I had been extra paranoid ever since Thugga had been hitting our shit and getting damn near everything. Kon and I had to switch shit up after finding out Don was a got damn traitor. I couldn't wait to get my hands on that motherfucker and make his ass pay for that shit.

Every time I walked out of the door, Sa'nai was paranoid as hell thinking I wasn't going to come back through that motherfucker. I had to keep telling her that I was straight. I knew there was a fucking threat out there and was more cautious. She wasn't hearing that shit though.

A Challenger pulled up in front of the house. I couldn't figure out who the hell it was. I pulled my strap from my waistline and eased up from the chair I was sitting in. The driver's side door pushed open and Cam's head emerged.

Ever since my incident, he had been here with me. I knew he wasn't going anywhere until we got our hands on Don. The task was becoming fucking impossible. All of his regular spots, he was a got damn ghost. That nigga knew what the fuck he was doing when he fucking disappeared.

"What you doing, nigga?" Cam approached the porch and I passed him the blunt.

"Just sitting here thinking."

"'Bout what?"

"This whole shit with Don. I can't believe that mother-fucker traded on us."

"Believe it. I see that shit all the time up there in Tallahas-see. Niggas get greedy and fucking expect more."

"We were paying that nigga good though."

"Why don't you do something about the shit instead of sit-ting 'round here moping and shit like a lil' bitch."

"I been tryna do something 'bout it. I can't find that nigga anywhere."

"You driving off emotions nigga." He took another pull from the blunt and passed it to me. "Find the shit the nigga love most and take that shit away from him. If he doesn't come out, then I don't know what to tell you."

"That nigga doesn't love shit. He been with Kon and me since he was 'bout eleven years old."

"See, that's where you're fucking wrong. I been doing my re-search and turns out, that lil' nigga got a lil' bitch on the east side with a lil' Don junior."

I scratched my head. "How come I didn't know anything 'bout it?"

"'Cause he didn't want you to know about it."

"You know exactly where I can find her?"

"Thought you'd never ask." A smirk formed on his face. "Let's go."

Putting the blunt out, I followed him to his car. Cam took me to the east side and pulled up directly to her house.

"How the fuck you found out 'bout this?"

"I have my ways." He flashed me that infamous smirk of his and climbed out of his car. I got out behind him and observed as he checked the clip in his strap and slapped it back in. "So, how you want to handle this shit? You know I'm down for anything."

"I wanna see if we can get her to tell us where he is or at least get him to come to us. I don't want to go in there guns blazing and it be a waste of a fucking trip."

"Got it." He trekked up to the front door with me right on his heels. I really wanted to know how the fuck he got this information. This was my got damn city and I couldn't come across that information.

He tapped on the door with the barrel of his gun. I wasn't sure if anyone was at home, but if they weren't, I was prepared to wait there until someone returned. I had been letting Don run the streets for far too fucking long. It was time I put his ass to and end and get the got damn information I need to get my hands on Thugga. The sooner I handled his ass, the fucking better.

The door pulled open and this slim petite chick stood there with a little boy on her hip that looked to be about four years old. If that was Don's child, he did damn well at keeping him a secret for years. Maybe he didn't want anyone to know about them because of shit like this. He probably knew that he was going to do some fuck shit and didn't want it to come back on them.

"Can I help you?" Her eyes expanded when they landed on Cam's gun. I didn't take mine out because I didn't need it at the moment.

"I'm looking for Don's baby mama. Are you her?"

Her eyes traveled from Cam to me, then back to him. I could tell she was frightened from the tremble of her body.

"It's okay. Can we come in?"

"F-for what?"

"I need to talk to you 'bout something."

"Whatever it is, I don't know anything."

Without uttering another word, I pushed my way into the house. It was nice on the inside. Looked like she should have been an interior decorator of some sort. I wasn't sure how she got mixed up with a nigga like Don. She looked straight out of his fucking league. Baby girl was beautiful as hell.

She had long flowing black hair with a beauty mark underneath her left eye. She wore these black square framed glasses. For her to be tiny as hell, she had a nice shape to her.

"You can make this shit really simple or we can do it the hard way," Cam spoke up. I cut my eyes at him. That nigga was trigger happy and I just wanted to make this shit as clean as possible. Shorty didn't have to die. The only person I was really after was Don's ass.

"Wha-what is he talking about?" Her eyes quickly shot to mine.

"I know you know where Don is." I got comfortable on her couch and she held onto her son a little bit tighter.

"If you want him so bad, why don't you just go to his job?"

"Job?" Cam quizzed with a chuckle. "That nigga ain't got no fucking job."

"Yes, he does," she replied confidently. I wasn't sure what the fuck Don had been telling her, but that nigga has never worked a fucking job a day in his got damn life.

"Listen baby girl, I'm pretty sure that you know just like we know, Don ain't got no fucking job."

"Yes, he does. He works for a delivery company."

Cam chortled and pulled a pack of cigarettes from his pocket. I cut my eyes at him and put them back on shorty.

"What company?" Her lips parted, but they quickly shut.

"I know that face from anywhere. That's the face a woman makes when she realizes her nigga been fucking lying to her." Cam placed a cigarette into his mouth and went to light it.

"Can you not do that in here. My son is present."

Cam's eyes landed on me. I nodded and he excused himself

outside.

"Can you tell me what's going on?" Her body relaxed when he was no longer in the room. I guess she figured that she was safer with me. If she cooperated, she wouldn't have a damn thing to worry about. Sure, she'd be raising her child alone, but that's better than being fucking dead.

"All I want is Don. You don't have anything to worry 'bout if you just hand that nigga over."

"But I don't know where he is."

"Call him."

She glanced down at her son with teary eyes. In that moment, she realized that he'd never see his father again.

"Can I take him to his room first?"

"Sure, but I'm coming with you."

Rising to my feet, I followed her down the hallway to make sure she wasn't going to try any slick shit. She placed him down on his feet and kissed him on top of his head.

"Mommy will be right back. Be good."

She eased past me to the doorway and grabbed the knob. I stepped out into the hallway and she shut the door behind us.

"May I ask what he did?"

"Ratted out the only fucking family he had to the got damn enemy."

"You're going to kill him, aren't you?"

"Just do whatever it takes to get his ass over here."

Her head lowered and she slipped her phone from her back pocket of her pants. I watched closely as she scrolled down to his name and pressed dial.

"Put it on speaker."

Her gaze met mine and I mugged her. She did as she was told

and we both listened to the phone chime until it picked up.

"Yeah, bae?"

Her eyes bucked and I nodded.

Clearing her throat, she said, "Where are you?"

"I'm at work. You know this. Is everything okay?"

She hesitated for a moment.

"I thought you paid the car note. You know those people are outside trying to take my car?" I was shocked at how quickly that lie rolled off her tongue. She was smart; I could give her that. Any other bitch would try to be that nigga's ride or die, and fucking get killed trying to warn him and shit.

"Are you fucking serious?" I could sense the anger in his voice.

"Yeah, I tried talking to him, but he didn't want to hear shit I had to say. He even got a lil' rough with me."

"Hold that nigga there as long as you can. I'm on my fucking way." The call disconnected and she locked eyes with me.

"I did what you want. Can you promise not to hurt my son? He's only three. You can do whatever you want with me, just don't hurt my son." Moisture filled her eyes. I'm not sure what gave her the bright ass idea that I was going to do something to her. I had no interest in hurting her. She did everything I asked, so there really was no point.

"Long as you keep cooperating, you don't have shit to worry 'bout." I snatched her phone from her grips, so she wouldn't try to send Don a text of some shit to warn him. She may have been doing everything I wanted her to, but that didn't mean she wouldn't sneak and do some shit.

"Thank you."

Nodding, I shoved her toward the living room. Cam was back in there, comfortable as fuck with his feet propped up and a fucking sandwich in his hand. No matter who's house we went over, that motherfucker made himself comfortable.

"Damn, y'all was back there fucking or something?" he asked, taking a bite of his sandwich.

"Don's on his way." Rounding the table, I slapped his feet down and took a seat next to him. Shorty eased down in the chair adjacent to us. I observed her as she fiddled with her fingers. From the sweat beads on her forehead, I could tell she was uncomfortable as shit.

We sat there a good forty-five minutes before Don made his grand entrance. The locks clicked and I quickly pulled my strap from my waistline.

"Go in the room with your son," I whispered to her and she jetted out of there. I didn't want her to see what was about to happen to her baby daddy. I could tell she was innocent and didn't want to fuck up her mind. She kind of reminded me of Sa'nai. She was innocent and sweet once upon a time. After I got shot, all that shit vanished.

The door pushed open and I saw the side of Don's face. My dick grew hard in my pants because I was finally about to get something I had been yearning for for the longest.

"Ashley?" he called out shorty's name and shut the door. His gaze met mine when he heard my gun cock. "What the fuck are y'all doing here and what did you do with Ashley?" His hands balled into fists, but I wasn't worried about him putting his got damn hands on me. He was outnumbered and out gunned.

"If you weren't hiding like a lil' bitch, we wouldn't be here," Cam spoke up.

"Who the fuck are you?"

"Don't worry 'bout all that," I told him. "You gon' tell me every fucking thing I wanna know 'bout that nigga Thugga."

"I ain't telling you shit, and if you hurt Ashley or my got

damn chi—"

"What the fuck you gon' do?" Cam rose from the couch. He already wanted to place a hot one in Don's ass for shooting me, so he was treading on thin ice. Him threatening us wasn't helping him at all.

"It's cool." I lifted my hand, stopping Cam from dropping that nigga where the fuck he stood.

Nearing Don, I sensed his uneasiness. He talked like he was all hard and shit, but he was weak at the moment. The one thing he feared losing the most, he could lose forever if he made the wrong move. Little did he know, I didn't kill children. I'd lay a bitch down if I had to, but children were off limits.

"You already know how I get down. Just do the shit the easy way. You gon' die either way. Wouldn't you rather it be quick and painless?"

He stared me directly in the eyes and said, "Give me your best shot 'cause I ain't telling you shit."

"Fine; have it yo' way."

Wham!

I hit his ass straight across the face with the butt of my gun. Blood seeped from the corner of his mouth.

"Kick his ass," I instructed Cam and sat down in the chair Ashley was in before I made her leave the room.

"With pleasure." Popping his neck, Cam neared Don. I sat there watching him as he beat the shit out of that nigga. Don's face was bloody and battered. His eyes were damn near swollen shut.

Cam kicked him hard in the ribs and looked back in my direction. Lifting my hand, I halted him.

"You still don't have shit to say?"

Coughing up a mouth full of blood, he spit it on the floor and eyed me. "I'm still not telling you shit."

Any other nigga probably would have broken his fucking neck to tell me what I wanted to know if I was sitting in their shit threatening their fucking life with their family in the next room. It made me really wonder if he gave a fuck about them in the first place.

Gripping him by the collar of his shirt, Cam shoved the barrel of his gun into the side of his dome.

"You really think you're big and bad 'cause you fucking outsmarted us the first time, but that shit won't ever happen again. You tryna be loyal to a nigga that you barely even fucking know. You think that nigga gives a fuck 'bout you. He using yo' dumb ass 'cause you beneficial to him."

"I'm still not telling you shit."

From the mug on his face, I knew he was serious. With a nod of the head, Cam sent a bullet crashing through Don's head. There was no point in sitting around trying to get him to talk when I knew he wasn't. In all of the time that I'd known him, he'd never been a snitch, so I didn't quite understand how the fuck Thugga was able to turn him against us in the first fucking place.

Pulling my phone out, I dialed the clean-up crews' number. As the phone rang in my ear, sobbing could be heard coming from behind me. Turning around, I saw Ashley standing there with tears streaming down her cheeks. That wasn't some shit I wanted her to see and if she would have stayed her ass in the room like I told her to, then she wouldn't have witnessed some bullshit like that.

"I'm 'bout to shoot you my location. Get someone over here as soon as possible," I said, disconnecting the call. I swiftly shot them a text to let them know where I was. Turning back to Cam, I said, "They on the way to clean this shit up. I'm 'bout to head out."

"What 'bout her?" He nodded in Ashley's direction.

"I'm sure she won't say shit."

"What makes you so sure 'bout that?" His brow rose as he stared at me.

"She helped us get Don. I'm sure she's smart enough not to say shit unless she wants to end up like the motherfucker." I cut my eyes at her and hers were glued to Don lying on the floor in a puddle of his own blood. I was confident that she wasn't a got damn threat. If I got the slightest inkling that she was going to be one, I'd be right back at her door with a bullet with her fucking name on it.

"Aight, but don't say I didn't tell you so."

I left out of the door, leaving Cam in there to handle that shit. I forgot that I rode there with him, so I had to hit up Brock to come scoop me and take me back to my car.

After picking my car up, I went straight home. I felt a thousand times better now that I had gotten Don's ass off the fucking street, but I still needed to find that motherfucker Thugga. He was making it impossible as hell for us to handle business. I hated that we had to switch shit up the way we did and lost out on some business. I didn't want to let a lot of people know where the new traps were located too terrified that Thugga was going to find out about those as well.

We had spent so much fucking money replacing the shit he and Don had been stealing from us.
If I could bring that motherfucker back to life and kill him all over again, then I would. That nigga caused us too much fucking problems.

Getting out of the car, I entered the house and garlic immediately attacked my nostrils. Sa'nai was in the kitchen cooking something. I went in there and grabbed a bottle of D'USSÈ and immediately turned it up.

"You okay?" she asked over her shoulder and went back to stirring something in a pot.

"I finally got the nigga that shot me."

"Are you serious!" She swiftly turned on her heels, facing me and I could hear the excitement in her voice.

"Yeah." I turned the bottle up again.

"That's great isn't it?" She neared me.

"Yeah. I just wish that I could have gotten more information out of his ass than I did."

"I know you're still trying to get that guy and you will when the time is right. Don't stress yourself about it." Getting on her tippy toes, she pecked me on the lips.

"Thanks."

"Thanks for what?" She frowned up at me.

"For all that you do." Bracketing her waist, I pulled her into my frame and gazed down into her eyes.

"You know I got your back."

"And I love you for that shit."

"Now, get your stanky ass up there and get cleaned up, so we can eat dinner."

"You know you love my funk." I chuckled and she playfully hit me on the arm.

I stared at her for a moment as she took the food out of the oven. I still couldn't believe she made a nigga fall for her ass and had me in a whole relationship. Sa'nai was probably the best thing that ever happened to me and I was going to do whatever it fucking took to keep her.

Kon

I was happy as fuck for Blessed when he told me he finally got Don's stupid ass. It frustrated me that he wasn't able to get any intel on Thugga's ass. That nigga had taken so much shit from me that it was crazy. I couldn't wait to get my hands on that motherfucker, so he could pay.

Sapphire had been spending a lot of time with Stormie whenever she didn't have to work. I loved seeing those two together. Stormie was going to need a motherly figure since Chrissy's dumb ass was no longer in the picture.

Since Sapphire had to work, I left the warehouse earlier to go pick Stormie up from school. Normally, if I was working, I'd depend on Blessed to get her or let her catch a ride home with Sa'nai, but I was trying to stop depending so heavily on them. I knew they were about to bring a seed into this world and was going to have a lot or responsibility of their own. Blessed was happy as hell that he was about to be a father. I still couldn't believe Chrissy was so fucking salty about me leaving her that she took my chance of being a father again away from me.

I snapped from my thoughts when I saw the children emerging from the building. I searched them for Stormie, but didn't see her anywhere. I sat there in my car for a good ten minutes and pulled my phone out to call Sapphire to see if she left work early or something and picked her up. If she had, she usually would have told me something like that.

"Hey, bae. I was just about to call and ask what y'all wanted for dinner."

"Y'all?"

"Yeah, you and Stormie, silly. Who else?"

"You mean to tell me she's not with you?"

"Oh, my God. Please don't tell me she's missing again."

I hopped from the car and entered the small crowd of children that were lingering in front of the front steps.

"Hope not. Let me go see if she's still in here with Sa'nai."

"Call me and let me know. If not, I'll leave work and help you search for her."

"Okay."

Disconnecting the call, I slipped my phone into my pocket and entered the building, going straight to Sa'nai's classroom. It just wasn't like Stormie to not be in place for someone to pick her up. After what happened the last time when she went missing, I was worried sick about her.

Stopping at Sa'nai's classroom door, I peeked into the room and saw that Stormie was still sitting at her desk with Sa'nai kneeled down alongside her. Tears streamed down Stormie's cheeks.

"What's going on?" I asked, fully entering the classroom.

Sa'nai's head snapped in my direction and she locked eyes with me. "She's just upset about Chrissy."

I slowly neared Stormie's desk and she dried her eyes with her hands. I hated that I had to lie to her about her mother, but it was the only way I was going to be able to keep the peace between us.

"What's wrong, baby girl?" I questioned, kneeling down alongside her.

Her gaze met mine and I could feel her pain. For the longest, she had been doing just fine. Of course, she was upset when she first found out about her mother being dead. I didn't expect for her to get over it so quickly. The guilt was fucking eating me up inside and causing me to drink even more than ever. That along with the bullshit going on with Thugga. That nigga needed to be caught immediately before he became an even bigger issue.

"I miss my mama."

"I know, baby." I gently stroked her tears from her eyes with my fingertips. "I know you're probably hurting right now, but I promise you that everything's gon' get better."

Her arms quickly wrapped around my neck. I scooped her up from the desk and grabbed her book bag.

"If there's anything I can do to help, just let me know," Sa'nai made known as I made my way toward the door.

"Thanks."

I took Stormie outside and placed her into the car. Climbing into the driver's seat, I started the car and pulled from my parking spot. I instantly called Sapphire back to let her know that everything was all right. I didn't want her to get too worked up about Stormie.

"Did you find her?" she quickly answered the phone, not even giving me time to say anything.

"Yeah, she was still in the classroom with Sa'nai." My eyes shifted to the rearview mirror at Stormie who was in the back-seat, scrolling her tablet. "She's upset about Chrissy. I don't know what to do."

"You could just tell her the truth."

"I don't think that'll be the best idea." I didn't want to cause her even more pain.

"Well, I'm going by the store right now to grab something to cook for dinner. I'll meet you back at the house."

"Okay." I disconnected the call. "You good back there?"

Stormie sniffled and nodded. Deep down, I knew my child would never be good again. Losing someone such as a parent did something to a person. They carried that grief with them for the rest of their life. I should have thought about that shit before placing that bullet in Chrissy's head, but it wasn't anything I could do about it.

∞∞∞

After I dropped Stormie off at home, I found myself leaving to think. All of this shit was becoming too much for me.

I sat there at the bar, tossing back my D'USSÉ, shot after shot. I had been sitting there for so long that I lost count of how many drinks I had. It was getting late and Sapphire had been blowing up my phone nonstop until she killed the fucking battery.

"I think you've had enough. I'm about to call you an Uber," the bartender said, but I wasn't trying to hear that shit. I had come there to forget about everything for a moment.

"Let me get another one."

"I'm not giving you anything. I think you should go home, Kon," she said.

"Fine, whatever." I slammed the shot glass down on the bar and it shattered.

Getting up from the barstool, I stumbled a little bit.

"I'm calling you an Uber. You don't need to be driving like that."

"I—I'm good. I don't need no fucking Uber."

"You don't need to be fucking driving."

Waving her off, I staggered out of the bar and hit the fob on my car. Getting inside, I pulled out of the parking lot. I was on the road for about five minutes before hearing the police siren and seeing flashing lights behind me.

Scrubbing my hand down my face, I pulled over to the side of the road. *Maybe I should have taken that got damn Uber.*

I glanced back at the car in the rearview mirror and watched as he sat in the car. I wasn't sure what the fuck he was doing, but he needed to let me know what he fucking pulled me over for.

The driver's door pushed open and he climbed out, nearing my car. My heart rate quickened, knowing I had been drinking and hoped the shit wasn't obvious. The last thing I needed was to get in fucking trouble with the got damn police.

I winded the window down and flashed him a fake ass smile. "Can I help you, Officer?"

"You know you were swerving?"

"Was I really?" My brow arched. I thought I was focused as shit and doing an excellent job at driving. That nigga probably saw me leave the bar and wanted to fucking fuck with me.

Leaning his head toward the window, he sniffed. "Have you been drinking?"

"I had a little, but it wasn't that much."

Clutching his strap, he took a step back. "I'm going to have to ask you to step out of the vehicle."

"For what?"

"You've been drinking."

"I'm not getting out of my car. Can you tell me the real reason why you pulled me over? Was it 'cause I was driving while black?"

"I'm going to ask you one more time, step out of the vehicle."

"Fine whatever." I sighed, getting out of the car.

He gripped me by the wrist and bent it behind my back. The

shit happened so fucking fast, I didn't know what the fuck was going on.

"What the hell are you arresting me for?"

"You smell like you've drink an entire bottle of liquor."

"You got to be fucking kidding me."

I didn't utter another word, just allowed him to pull me over to the police car and place me in the back. I knew that I wasn't going to be in that motherfucker long, so I might as well had gone on without a hassle.

∞∞∞

"White!" the officer yelled waking me from my sleep. I shot up on the bench and gazed at the bars as he approached them. "You've made bail." The door buzzed and I rose to my feet. I wasn't sure who had come and got me because they wouldn't even let me have my first phone call. The motherfuckers kept saying I was acting disorderly and told me to sleep the liquor off.

I followed him to the desk and signed my paperwork, then I was free to go. When I stepped out the doors, I saw Von standing beside his car. If he was standing before me, then I knew that couldn't be a good thing. Von was my father and also my supplier. He stood back and allowed me to run my organization how I saw fit. I tried to keep him out of the whole Thugga ordeal, but once all my shit kept coming up missing, I had no other choice than to let him know what the hell was going on.

"What's up?" I said to him, nearing his car.

"What's up?" He mugged me, peeling his tall, lean frame from the car. "I bail yo' sorry ass out of jail and all you can fucking offer me is fucking what's up?"

"I wasn't trying to get locked up. I had one too many drinks and that cop from last night was on fuck shit. That nigga didn't even know I was got damn drunk 'til he fucking pulled me over. That motherfucker followed me all the way from the bar just to get me."

"It don't matter. You supposed to be on yo' got damn toes with that shit going on out there with that motherfucker Thugga. I thought you would have handled that shit by now. Don't tell me that I'm gon' have to step in and take care of the shit myself."

I clenched my teeth. And there he was, that motherfucker couldn't wait for me to got damn fuck up, so he could come in and play the fucking hero. That's the shit he did. Since I wanted to branch out and do my own shit, he'd been waiting for me to fucking fail, so he could swoop in and call himself saving me.

"I don't need yo' help. I can handle the shit on my own."

"If you don't take care of that fucking problem within the next couple of days, I'm gon' do the shit for you. Now, get in the got damn car."

He yanked his car door open and slipped inside. Sighing, I climbed in alongside him. My phone began ringing. Glancing down, I saw it was Blessed calling me.

"Yeah?"

"You not gon' believe this shit."

"What happened?" My heart thumped rapidly in my chest. I couldn't wait to see what he was going to say.

"You know that nigga Chrissy was staying with?"

"What 'bout him?"

"That was Thugga."

"You fucking lying."

"Nope. Meet me at the warehouse right quick and we'll explain everything to you."

"Bet." Ending the call, I glanced over at Von. His eyes peered at me.

"What happened?"

"Blessed found out how we gon' get Thugga."

"And how y'all supposed to do that?"

"I'on know. Drop me off at my car right quick."

"Just remember what I said... a couple of days."

I brushed off that bullshit Von was talking. He was putting even more pressure on my ass to handle Thugga and I wasn't feeling that bullshit.

It was all beginning to make sense now. How Thugga was able to hit most of my shit and knew my fucking moves. Chrissy's dumbass was telling that nigga every fucking thing he wanted to know. If I wasn't glad she was six feet under, I damn sure was fucking glad now.

I made it to the warehouse quicker than usual. Probably because my mind was all over the place and my fucking trigga' finger was itching. I couldn't wait to get my got damn hands on Thugga. That motherfucker thought he was smart as hell.

I entered the warehouse to see what the hell was going on.

"Blessed!" I barked his name to see where the hell he was.

"I'm in the office," he yelled back.

Entering his office, weed attacked my nostrils. I noticed a guy sitting in a chair in front of his desk with a blunt dangling from his lips.

"Who the fuck is this?"

"Kon, this is Brick. The nigga that's gon' lead us straight to Thugga.

"Who this nigga supposed to be and why the fuck he in here?" Blessed of all people should have known how fucking paranoid I was after Thugga damn near found everything I had worked so fucking hard to build. I never let strangers into the warehouse, so I didn't understand how come this nigga was sitting in front of me now. Yeah, he lost his fucking mind.

"He used to work for Thugga. It's how I found out Chrissy was staying with him. He agreed to help us take his ass down."

"And why the fuck would he want to do that?"

"Let's just day we got the same common enemy," Brick spoke up as if someone asked him some shit.

"What makes you think I believe you really wanna help us get Thugga. Have you ever thought this shit could be a fucking trap?" I asked Blessed. He was so in a rush to take Thugga down that he wasn't thinking clearly.

"It's not. That motherfucker killed my got damn girl 'cause I didn't do something he wanted me to. I think it's 'bout time we send that nigga to meet his maker."

"Sounds like a plan to me." Blessed rubbed his hands together.

Nearing Blessed's desk, I grabbed his piece and shoved it into the side of Brick's head. "If I get the slightest feeling that you're on some bullshit, I'ma put a got damn bullet in your fucking head."

"Promise you don't have anything to worry 'bout," he replied.

"Aight, so how we gon' do this?" I questioned them and a smirk appeared on Blessed's face.

"It's as simple as taking candy from a baby. Brick already got a meeting set up with the nigga."

"Don't you think Thugga would think something's off if he knows he killed his girl?" The shit wasn't making any sense to me.

"He thinks that I don't know it was him who killed Alicia. I set up a meeting to talk to him about getting more product in a trap. Once the nigga gets to the house, y'all can do whatever the fuck you want to with him."

"What you waiting for? Let's go." I was beyond ready to get this shit over with.

Slipping Blessed's gun back on his desk, I slid it over to him. I stopped by my office to grab my strap on my way out of the door.

It took us no time to make it to the trap house where Thugga was supposed to meet Brick. He took us inside and we sat there waiting for Thugga to arrive. Brick peeked out the window and my eyes shifted to Blessed who was sitting across from me on the love seat. His eyes were glued to his phone as his fingers went swiftly across his screen with a stupid ass smirk on his face. I was quite sure he was probably texting Sa'nai's ass.

It reminded me about the way I left shit with Sapphire because I was in such a rush to take care of this shit. I had to take care of things with her and Stormie when I was done.

"There he goes!" Brick quickly turned to us and we rose from the couch. "Go into the room right there." He pointed at a door. I swore everything about this shit felt off as fuck to me, but I rushed into the room anyway. I was going to give his ass enough time to make it into the house and get comfortable. After that, I had a fucking bullet with his got damn name on it.

"You better hope this shit works," I whispered to Blessed as we stood in the bedroom like two niggas that had snuck in a bitch's house and her nigga came home early.

"It will," he assured me.

"What the fuck you called me out here for, Brick, when you haven't even gotten the shit off I just gave you? I swear you niggas be just wasting my motherfuckin' time."

"It ain't even like that. I already moved that shit." I heard the front door close, then footsteps passed the door. A few seconds later, there was a thud sound. "There's your money right there."

"How the fuck you got that shit off that fast?"

"Let's just say I have my ways."

I glanced in Blessed's direction. That shit had his name written all over it. He shrugged his shoulders.

"Aight, so what you want now?"

"I—" Before he could finish his sentence, I burst out of the room. I was over waiting.

"The fuck going on?" he quizzed as his eyes landed on me.

"You thought you were gon' get away with fucking with me?" My hand rose and my gun aimed directly at his head, so he wouldn't be able to do shit.

"Really? You helping these motherfuckers?" Thugga mugged Brick and he took a step back.

"You even stooped as fucking low as using Chrissy." Heat coursed through my veins. I had been waiting so long to stand in front of this motherfucker.

"Chrissy was fucking easy. I didn't even have to fuck the bitch to get any information. She was that fucking desperate to fuck you over."

My hand tightened around my strap.

Pow!

I shot his ass in the fucking shoulder.

"Ahh!" he hollered.

"If I had known you were the one she was staying with, I would have stayed and put a bullet in yo' ass then."

His eyes narrowed as he gazed at me. "So, what? You 'bout to kill me?"

"Damn right." My gun shifted to his forehead.

"You kill me, and you'll have every fucking cop in Miami beating your fucking door down."

"No, I won't. I'ma hide yo' motherfuckin' ass."

"I think they'll notice when one of their own goes missing."

"Nigga, you a got damn cop!" Blessed questioned him and he eyed him.

"Let 'em motherfuckin' come."

"But don't you wanna know why I did the shit in the first place?"

I knew the motherfucker was only trying to buy fucking time, but I played into his bullshit anyway to see what the fuck he had to say.

"Why?"

"You killed my father and took everything away from my family. Did you really think you were going to get away with the shit?"

"What the hell are you talking 'bout? Titan?"

"Who else?" He mugged me and suddenly, everything made sense. I always wondered how come he was after me in the first fucking place. That nigga just appeared out of the fucking blue and came gunning for me. I killed Titan so fucking long ago and he suddenly decided he wanted to get fucking revenge. He probably had plenty of time to plot against me.

"I killed Titan and now I'm 'bout to kill you."

Pow!

I sent a bullet crashing straight through his fucking skull.

"Let's get the fuck out of here," I told Blessed treading toward the door.

"Y'all gon' let me keep the money?" Brick quickly asked.

"Hell nah," I answered, sending a bullet straight through his fucking heart.

"What you do that for?" Blessed questioned me.

"I ain't trust the motherfucker. Text the clean-up crew," I

told him as he picked up the duffel and trekked behind me out of the door.

On my way to the house, I gazed at the million text messages I had from Sapphire. She was worried sick since I hadn't been home since the day before and she hadn't heard anything from me. I was meaning to call her when I got out of jail, but Blessed threw me off track. I was happy as fuck that we finally dealt with Thugga's ass and I didn't have to fucking worry about him again.

Sapphire: *Lace came and got Stormie. I just thought you should know even though you haven't been answering the fucking phone.*

Me: *After I pick her up, I'm on my way to the house and I'll explain what happened.*

Too much shit had transpired for me to try and tell her through text message. I hit a u-turn in the street and went straight for Lane's house. She hadn't said anything about picking Stormie up. I didn't mind her hanging with her or anything, but I felt like it was strange as fuck for her to come and pick her up out of the got damn blue.

Pulling in front of the house, I climbed out of the car and went up to the front door. It took Lane no time to answer it with a smug expression on her fucking face.

"What the fuck you looking like that for?"

"I told Stormie you killed Chrissy."

"You did what!" My eyes damn near bulged from my fucking sockets. A smirk appeared on her face and the shit pissed me the fuck off even more. I rammed my gun into the side of her dome and that smirk quickly faded.

"She deserved to know the truth."

"That didn't give you the right to fucking tell it to her."

"Yes, it did. She's my granddaughter and that was my child you made me lay to rest."

"Chrissy knew what the fuck she was getting her ass into

when she fucking stabbed Sapphire and put her got damn hands on Stormie." I don't know what the fuck she thought was going to happen when I found out what the fuck was going on. I let Chrissy off the hook one too many times and that was the reason her ass was out of hand.

"So, what you gon' do? Kill me too?"

Sinking my teeth into my lower lip, I dropped my hand and backed away from her. "As much as I fucking want to... no. Stormie is already pissed the fuck off with me. I'm not about to make her even mangrier.

"She deserved to know the truth about her mother, Kon. It was best she found out now instead of down the line. You think she was mad with you now, if you let years slip by without telling her, she probably would never speak to you again."

"I don't think she is now." I scrubbed my hand down my face. I couldn't be angry with anyone but myself. No one made me pull that fucking trigger. I pulled it because I wanted to.

"She'll get over it soon or later."

"You better fucking hope she does."

Storming into Stormie's bedroom, I locked eyes with her. She stood to her feet and glared at me with her head tilted.

"Come on, Stormie, we're leaving."

"Did you hurt mama?"

I cut my eyes at Lane who was standing in the doorway with her arms folded over her chest.

"No, grandma don' t know what she's talking about."

"But she said you hurt mama."

"I didn't do anything to your mama. Isn't that right, Lane." My eyes darted in her direction and she fixed her mouth to say something, but then closed it as if she had to think about what was about to fly from her fucking lips.

"He's right. He didn't do anything."

"But how come you—"

"I don't know why she lied about that."

Stormie stared at Lane for a moment, then shrugged her shoulders.

"Can we have pizza for dinner?"

"You can have whatever you want, princess." Gripping her by the hand, I led her out of the bedroom, mugging Lane. I wanted to do something to that woman, but I didn't want another death on my conscious eating me the fuck alive.

Sapphire

The next day

Rolling over in bed, I noticed Kon was no longer beside me. Tossing the cover back, I climbed out of bed and went into the bathroom to handle my hygiene. When I was done, I got dressed and sauntered down the hallway to get a late breakfast started. Normally, I would have been up and had the food already on the table before we got ready to leave the house, but I was off today and decided to sleep in for a little bit.

Entering the kitchen, I grabbed everything from the fridge that I was going to need and placed it on the counter. I fumbled in the cabinet to get the pans. By the time I set one down on the stove, I heard someone come through the front door. I knew it was Kon. Anger consumed me. I knew he had been fucking avoiding me, but I didn't know why.

The day before when he brought Stormie home, he turned right around and left out of the house again. I wasn't sure where he had gone, but he had some got damn explaining to do.

"Kon!" I shouted at the top of my lungs. A few moments later, he appeared in the doorway. "Where the hell you been at?"

"I had to go meet with my father."

"And it took you all fucking night to do that shit. You still ain't fucking told me where the hell you were yesterday and the day before."

"I got arrested for a DUI and my Pops came and bailed me out. He was on my ass 'bout this Thugga shit, so I handled it."

I poured my eggs into the skillet and scrambled them. "You disappear on me like that again, we gon' have a fucking problem."

"You don't have shit to worry 'bout." His arm bracketed my waist, and he pecked me on the cheek. "I'm 'bout to go get cleaned up. I'll be back down for breakfast."

Smack!

He smacked me on the ass and disappeared upstairs.

∞∞∞∞

Later that day

I missed my doctor's appointment the day before because I didn't know where the fuck Kon was and I was damn near panicking. I couldn't miss my appointment this time around. Since Kon was back home, I wanted to stay there with him, but I decided against it. Hopefully, he'd be there by the time I made it back.

"Sapphire?" Dr. Georgia said, bringing me from my thoughts. They had me sitting in that exam room for what seemed like fucking hours. I had completely zoned the fuck out.

"Yeah, sorry." I gave her my undivided attention. The sooner she told me what the hell was going on with me, the sooner I could get the fuck out of there.

"Sorry it took me so long. I got your results right here." She gazed down at the blood work the nurse had taken prior to me coming in. "It says that you're pregnant. Congratulations." She flashed me a smile and my heart damn near dropped to the pit of my stomach.

"You sure that's right?"

"Yes."

"Let me see that." Sprouting to my feet, I snatched the

paper away from her. There was a lot of shit on there that I couldn't read. but I didn't miss the word pregnant as it stared back at me.

"How's this even possible?"

"Is that a serious question?" she quizzed me. My eyes stayed glued to the paper. After the shit that happened with Chrissy, I never thought about being pregnant again. It kind of fucking terrified me. All sorts of bad ideas immediately began running through my mind.

"I—I have to go." Without uttering another word, I zoomed for the door.

"Sapphire!" She called out behind me, but I kept running. I had to get the hell out of there, so I'd be able to fucking think.

Climbing into my car, I sat there for a moment, trying to figure out exactly what I was going to do. If I was pregnant, then I had to tell Kon what was going on. With everything he had going on at the moment, I wasn't sure if that was good news or not. The only person I could talk to now was Sa'nai.

Instead of taking my ass home like I was going to do, I decided to pop up at her house to tell her what was going on. Starting my car, I backed out of my parking space. My mind went into overdrive now that I was alone.

The first time I was pregnant, I wasn't too thrilled about it. Once Chrissy stabbed me and took my baby, it was really the only thing I could think about. Maybe God was giving me a second chance to have what she took away from me.

With that incident, it had me thinking that I probably wasn't even worthy to have a child. I thought I was being pushed for something, but now, I knew that wasn't the case.

I arrived at Sa'nai's house in no time. When I got there, I used my key to let myself inside. I bumped into boxes sitting on the floor in the living room that was marked 'bathroom'.

"Nai!" I called out her name, glancing at the other boxes stacked all over the living room. I wasn't sure what the fuck was going on, but I damn sure was about to find out.

"What you hollering my name like that for?" Her voice

bounced from her bedroom.

Entering her room, it was a complete fucking mess. She had clothes lying around everywhere. Shoes were thrown all over the fucking floor as if a tornado had swept through the motherfucker.

"What the hell you got going on? You moving or something?"

Her eyes peered back at me from her walk-in closet. "Yeah, Blessed asked me to move in with him. He thought it would be a great idea with us about to have a baby together.

"And you think that wasn't important enough to tell me? If I hadn't come by here, I probably wouldn't have known you were moving."

Standing, she slapped her hands together and exited the closet. "That's not true and you fucking know it."

"Yeah, whatever." I wasn't even in the mood to argue with her ass.

"Where you coming from anyway?" She took a swig of her Core water and sat down at the foot of her bed.

"The doctor."

"What did they say?" I had told Sa'nai all about how I hadn't been feeling too well lately. I was able to tell her that, that's why I didn't understand how come she hadn't found the time to let me know she was moving.

Taking a deep breath, I joined her on the bed. I knew I wasn't going to be able to deliver this news standing up. "I'm pregnant."

"Oh, my God! Congratulations, Sapphire!" Her arms quickly draped around my neck. I could tell she was excited as fuck for me, but I wasn't sure how Kon was going to feel about the situation. He was cool with it with the first pregnancy, but I didn't know how he would feel now.

"How come I feel like you're not excited about it?" she asked, pulling back from our embrace.

"No, I am, it's just, I don't know how to feel about it now. I'm kind of scared as fuck after what happened the last time I was pregnant."

"You don't have anything to worry about though. Chrissy's ass is dead now."

"I know…"

Her hand rested on my thigh and she squeezed it. "I understand that, but this is your second chance to be a mother. Embrace that shit."

"Yeah, you're right." A smile covered my face.

"Have you told Kon yet?"

"No."

"I'm sure he's going to be excited about it." She squealed, "Our babies are going to grow up together. I can't fucking wait! I wonder if they'll be close like us. What the fuck am I talking about?" She laughed. "Duh, they will be."

She was getting me all excited and shit about being pregnant. All the worries and butterflies I had when I found out I was about to be a mother, left my body.

"Just wait 'til the babies get here." She smiled brightly and got up from the bed. "You gon' help me finish packing or just sit there?"

"I shouldn't help you do shit since you didn't want to tell me you were moving in the first place." I got up from the bed and grabbed the tape off the dresser.

Sapphire

Epilouge

A month later

It had been an entire month since I found out I was pregnant. I was scared shitless at first, but Kon had been making everything a breeze. He catered to my every need. It didn't matter if I wanted the strangest shit or how late it was, he got up and made shit happen for me and I loved him for that.

Blessed and Sa'nai had been doing amazing. Their relationship was prospering, and I was so fucking happy for her. She was finally starting to show, and it was sinking deeper into her mind that she was about to be a mother. She was excited as hell that we both were pregnant at the same time.

Blessed had finally began to slowly let her in. She literally knew basically everything about this nigga. I don't even think I knew everything about Kon, but we had plenty of time to get there.

Lane had called herself coming around more after the shit she tried to pull with Kon. She should have known that shit wasn't going to fly with him when she tried that bullshit. Stormie had stopped asking about her mother. Shit was slowly trying to get back to normal. Kon was doing a whole lot better since he got rid of that Thugga character and I couldn't wait until everything was perfect again.

I had been busting my ass, pregnant and all, trying to get this new client's wedding all planned out by the date that they wanted it. It was hard trying to bounce back into my old ways of working all the time, but I was getting there.

It was the day of their wedding and I had everything already situated. I was placing the finishing touches on the reception hall, and then I was good to go.

"There you go," Sa'nai said, locking her arm with mine.

"What are you doing here?"

"Looking for you, silly."

She dragged me out of the reception hall and toward the room where the bride was supposed to have been getting ready in.

"Is something wrong?" I questioned her.

"No." Pushing the door in, I saw Amber standing there. She was supposed to have been getting ready for her wedding that started in an hour.

"How come you're not dressed?"

Panic set in. I just knew she was about to tell me that she was about to run out on the wedding. Whoever her husband was, he'd spent so much money on trying to give her the wedding of her dreams. Shit the motherfucker was the wedding of my got damn dreams. I was low-key hating and shit. If she ran out on that, she was crazy as hell.

"I've been waiting for you."

"For what?"

"This."

She unzipped the Vera Wang dress bag and the most gorgeous white mermaid gown gazed back at me.

"That dress is fucking beautiful."

I neared the dress with my mouth dropped to the floor. It was the most amazing thing I'd ever seen in my life. The beading around the heart-shaped neckline was impeccable.

"I'm glad you like it. Put it on."

"Wha-what?" I gazed at Amber as if she had two fucking heads.

Taking the dress out of the bag, she unzipped it from behind.

"She can't be serious," I said to Sa'nai.

"But she is." That was when I realized Sa'nai was dressed in a lavender cocktail dress.

"Are y'all going to tell me what the hell is going on?"

"Kon had you plan your own wedding. He thought it would be more romantic that way instead of proposing," Sa'nai said, tugging on my blazer.

Tears filled my eyes. I would have never guessed he'd do something like this. I never thought he would want to marry me. Marriage never came up in our discussions.

"What are you waiting for? You better get dressed before you're late," Sa'nai said, combing her fingers through my hair. "I'll grab Jason, so he can do something with this mess."

I was in awe, still not believing what was happening.

Before I knew it, I was dressed, and my hair was pulled up into an updo. I gazed at my reflection. I couldn't believe what I was seeing.

"You ready?" Sa'nai appeared at my side with a huge grin on her face.

"How could you keep something like this from me?" We told each other everything and she managed to keep this from me, knowing how I felt about surprises.

"He asked me not to say anything about it." She shrugged, placing my bouquet into my hand. "Let's get this show on the road."

We exited the room and I followed her to the white curtains. My heart rate quickened as I thought about seeing Kon at the end of the aisle. I couldn't wait to lay eyes on him.

Stormie appeared with a basket of white rose petals.

"You look so pretty, Sapphire."

"So, do you."

KC and JoJo's 'All my life' began playing and the curtains pulled back. Tears streaked my face as I stared at my family and friends as they stood to their feet. I didn't fuck with much people, so the ceremony was small. Most of the people there were people that Kon probably knew.

My eyes locked with his and I noticed tears forming in his eyes. Stormie pranced down the aisle, tossing the petals. Blessed stepped to Sa'nai's side and they began their stroll. I fanned my eyes and glanced in Amber's direction.

"What are you waiting for? Go get your man."

I strutted down the aisle to Kon. He loosened his tie and cleared his throat when I made it to him. My eyes bore into his. He grabbed my hands, placing a sweet kiss on the back of my left.

"I can't believe you did all this for me."

"I love the shit out of you, bae. I'd do anything for you."

"I love you too." Cupping his face, our lips meshed. His forehead pressed against mine and I stared deep into his eyes. "I'm pregnant."

"For real?" His eyes glistened, and right then, I knew that being with him was the best decision I could have possibly made.

The end.